St. Agnes' Place

a novel by Jill Starling

Dedicated to my special angels, Jamie, James and Matthew

In loving memory of my brother, Jimmy

Author's Note

Readers,

Although, I have never had to deal with child exploitation, I felt compelled to write a story that deals with this harrowing issue. Intimate details of those who have been lured into child sex trafficking in the United Stares have been carefully woven into my novel, thus presenting you with knowledge of this epidemic.

Since I began writing this novel, thankfully more attention has been given to this plight. Many states have passed the Safe Harbor Act, under which children who are too young to legally consent to sex would no longer be charged with prostitution and would no longer be treated as criminals. Instead, the courts would be required to provide counseling; medical assistance and the long-term shelter that would be needed in order for them to rebuild their lives. Modern day Mother Teresas such as Rachel Lloyd, Founder of Girls Educational and Mentoring Services (GEMS), and Rob Morris, President and Co-Founder of Love 146, and countless others continue to lead the fight to end modern day slavery.

Learning how to love again, friendship, redemption, and forgiveness are also recurring themes in this novel. I welcome you to St. Agnes' Place.

Enjoy!

Jill Starling

I felt ashamed and lost as I stared at the papers. It was now official: I was no longer the wife of a prominent attorney. I was a thirty-four year old woman without a child or career, and my only title was "Ex-Wife Of." Where did I fit in life's puzzle? I hadn't had this feeling since graduating from high school when I didn't have a clue what to do with my life. I had eventually decided to attend state college and major in accounting—or should I say my parents decided on that. I readily agreed since I had mastered the balance sheet in my high school business class. I met my first real love, Jonathon Massaconi, at a college dorm party and we were immediately smitten with each other. After graduating in the top five percent of my class, I took a job with a small company, balancing its books to help put Jon through law school. Jon eventually opened his own law firm and became the "go-to guy" for all the local politicians. I worked at home, taking care of the financial end of the business. We were financially well off, with plans of adopting a child and we were very happy, or so I thought.

Jon found his new normal with his twenty-something assistant whom I had the privilege of meeting and whom I had even liked. Stacey was brazen, beautiful and ready to take on the world, along with my wealthy husband. Never in a million years had I thought Jon would cheat on me or that I would see my marriage come to an end. I was wrong on both counts. I had never felt depression as powerful as this. Getting off the couch for at least an hour a day became my ultimate goal.

"I think you should go look for a job," my mother said as she sat across from me on the couch.

"I don't think a job is an option for me right now. I don't even want to take a shower."

"In time you will get through this. God doesn't give us anything we can't handle," she said, trying her best to reassure me.

As I continued to wallow in despair, I came to the realization that time doesn't necessary heal. It does force one to realize how pathetic one really can become. Thankfully, as weeks went by, I found solace through family, faith and the few good friends that I had. I came to realize you never know how strong you are until you no longer have a choice.

Jon sent a team to empty the house of all his belongings. He agreed to pay me alimony and sign over ownership of our condominium if I agreed to discontinue his bookkeeping. I readily agreed that he belonged to her now and that I should not be privy to his business records or to him in any way.

It was time to start anew, whether I wanted to or not. It was time to take off the sweatpants, brush my hair, and dab on some perfume. A season of change needed to take place.

****

"Why can't looking for a job on Craigslist be as exciting as looking for furniture or a date?" I thought as I scrolled through the employment listings. The economy was tight and most of the jobs available were for waitstaff. I knew the money wouldn't be what I was used to and those jobs were usually given to college students, not thirty-something ex-wives of. I also realized if I worked side by side with the younger generation, I would want to cause bodily harm to every pretty twenty-something who walked my way. A job in accounting would be ideal but they were scarce, and I knew it would be

too intense mentally for me to take on at this time. Scrolling down, I came across a job listing for a childcare specialist, with only a forwarding address. The listing contained no job description or phone number to call for inquiries. Something inside me told me to pursue this. I figured when you have absolutely nothing to lose, it's a good time to take a risk. I scribbled down the address: St. Agnes' Place, 54 South Allen Lane, Albany, New York 12205.

****

It was a sunny autumn day in Niskayuna, New York, a suburb in upstate New York, a day that made you want to walk outside, and crunch your feet on the crisp leaves and breathe the fresh air. I had nothing planned for the day, so I thought stopping by to inquire about the job listing would give me a reason to get out of the house. I made my way to the address, which was in the heart of Albany, not far from my suburban home. I made a turn off the main road and arrived at a cluster of old historic brick buildings. I parked my car and walked up the cobblestone path, not knowing where to turn. I must have looked like a mass of confusion as an older, stoic-looking, Hispanic woman with dark eyes and gray hair approached me.

"Can I help you?"

"Hi, I'm looking to speak with someone regarding the childcare specialist position."

"Well, you are talking to the right person. I'm Alma Valdez, the headmistress. You are in luck. I was just going for a stroll around the campus. Why don't you walk with me?"

We walked through garden after garden that had iron benches and plaques engraved with psalms. In the distance, I saw what looked like teenage girls playing kickball. Although the shrill noise of the game could be heard, there was a peaceful silence that echoed throughout the courtyard. We made our way down a path that led to an old Victorian home, which stood apart from the other brick buildings nestled upon the campus. It was pink with pale gray shutters and a wide-open, wraparound porch with tall white pillars. Directly in front of the house was a sign with a Norman Rockwell motif that read, "House of Love." Alma invited me in. The interior felt cozy and inviting. The living room had pastel-colored furniture, which was carefully arranged with beautiful crocheted afghans covering them. She led me to a large dining room table that was in full view of a kitchenette. Alma spoke with a strong, authoritative Hispanic accent.

"So, you are interested in working at St. Agnes' Place?"

"I am interested in a job, but I would like to know more about the position listed."

A sheepish grin played upon her lips as she explained, "We are a place of hope and safety for young girls who otherwise would be lost to the streets."

I was taken aback by her words, as I had imagined small children, swing sets and building blocks. Hesitantly, I remarked, "I thought this was some sort of school for young children."

"Oh, I am so sorry our ad was very vague, or shall I say rather useless. I sincerely apologize for your time."

"I would actually like to hear about the position."

Alma looked surprised and said, "What we do here at St. Agnes' Place is rescue, rehabilitate, and educate young women who have been forced into child trafficking."

I was shocked; I thought that only occurred in places like Africa, or Thailand. I thought of the young girls on the courtyard. They were just babies in my eyes.

"These girls look so young," I said sadly.

Alma remarked, "Unfortunately, they are. We work with the Department of Social Services, local police departments and the New York City Police Department, as well. These are vulnerable girls who have been picked up from bus stations, shopping malls, and while walking down their own streets. They are given material items, attention, and empty promises. Then the nightmare begins. They are kept isolated, threatened, and are repeatedly victimized. They are forced to service clients, or what they refer to as their Johns, while their captor, who is now their pimp, keeps all the money. The pimp will use whatever means necessary to keep the girl submissive. He will use physical force and intimidation. He makes them feel disgusting and ashamed, and many of them become hooked on drugs. The few who are found are given an opportunity to come here. Many are suicidal and have some sort of sexually-transmitted disease, and every one of them is dead inside. We take them away from their old environment and offer them a chance at a new life."

I could feel grief within me as I listened to Alma. "It must be so hard to raise a child in the city nowadays."

"Oh, but this problem is happening in the suburbs as well. It's in our own backyard, it's everywhere. Children from nice homes are just as susceptible. Where attention is given, children follow."

My voice started to raise a little as I asked, "What does this job entail?"

Alma smiled and her big brown eyes glistened as she stared intently at me. I felt as if she was looking into my soul as she spoke.

"We are in need of a dedicated individual to work nights and alternate weekends. That individual would assist the girls after their classes, eat dinner with them in the dining hall and help them with their homework. And at the end of the night they are to tuck them in at their new residence, this house we refer to on our campus as the "House of Love."

"The House of Love," how ironic, I thought.

Anxiously she asked, "How does this job sound to you now?"

"I must admit I have no experience working with young girls, but I think I would be up for the challenge."

"This position does require an incredible amount of patience and compassion."

I knew I had patience to a certain degree, sometimes too much compassion as Jon would often say, but I realize now compared to Jon, Hitler was compassionate.

"If you don't mind me asking Ms., I don't even think I asked you your name."

"Stevens," I answered. "Shawnsy Stevens," I stuttered almost forgetting that I no longer used the last name Massaconi.

"Miss Stevens, if you don't mind me asking–are you married, and do you have children of your own?"

I could feel the lump in my throat as I mumbled the words, "I have no children and I recently became divorced."

"I am sorry to hear that. The reason I ask is because this job also requires a strong degree of dedication."

"I have nothing going on in my life that would distract me."

"In that case," she said with a big grin, "The job is yours."

I looked at her, trying my best to conceal my surprise, and mumbled, "Thank you" as she extended her hand to mine.

"I will need you, though, to fill out some paperwork and I will need to do a background check. We also require drug testing."

"That's not a problem," I said, feeling somewhat overwhelmed, but excited.

"If everything checks out, you should be good to start in a couple of weeks."

Chapter 2

I anxiously waited all day with giddy delight to start my first day. The evening hours couldn't come quick enough. I felt like I was sixteen years old again and getting reading for my first job at Miller's Pharmacy. I arrived at the House of Love and was greeted by a plump, middle-aged woman with large rimmed glasses.

"Hi, I'm Wendy. I work the alternate shift and will be hanging with you for the week to help you out while you get a feel for things."

"I'm Shawnsy," I said with a feeling of relief. "I'm glad you're here because I really have no idea what I'm supposed to do."

With a warm smile that put me at ease, she said, "Just hang out, listen, and try not to let them get on your nerves. I hope you're hungry, because tonight we will be feasting on delicious pizza from Inferno Pizzeria, instead of going to the dining hall. I thought it would be easier, so you could have more time to get to know these lovely ladies, and for them to get to know you."

Wendy surveyed the room and pointed to each girl, as they were each involved in their own activities. "This is Keisha, Amy, Vicky and Leelee. Ladies, please welcome Miss Stevens."

They all turned around and muttered hello from their various stations.

"Hello, ladies. You can call me Shawnsy." The girls continued with their activities without acknowledgment.

Wendy gave me a reassuring glance and said, "Shawnsy, I am going to go order the pizza. Why don't you make yourself comfortable."

There was an awkward silence in the room. I felt as if I was being silently studied by each girl as I sat in the chair. Finally, the ice was broken.

"Why are you here?" Keisha asked, looking up from the books, notepads, stationary and envelopes that surrounded her at the dining room table.

Her strong voice, smooth mocha skin, and bright green eyes drew me in. It took me a moment to answer her, because at this point I was questioning this myself.

"I'm here to spend some time with you ladies and help you out with any of your needs. But most importantly, I am here to make sure that you feel safe and secure," I said feeling like I just read it off a cue card. They all looked at me with puzzled stares, which gave me the feeling I was a stranger in a foreign land.

"If you really want to keep us safe, why don't you help me write some letters?" Keisha asked.

"You want me to help you write some letters?" I asked.

"You said you wanted to keep us safe. I have a list of all the state legislators and I'm writing to them to pass the Safe Harbor Act."

I looked at her, confused, and asked, "What is that?"

"It's a law that hopefully will get passed that will keep girls like us who are under sixteen from being treated as criminals."

I was amazed at her determination, as she marked off her list and licked the envelopes.

"I would really love to help you out once I get settled. I think it's great that you are taking such initiative."

"Someday I want to be a lawyer," Keisha said proudly, while jotting in her notebook.

Amy looked up from the hip-hop magazine she was reading on the floor and said, "Keisha, you need a good lawyer."

Keisha said, "Shut up. Someday you'll be calling me to bail out your sorry ass."

Leelee, a petite Hispanic girl with long dark brown hair and dark eyes, was lying next to Amy on the floor while she doodled in her notebook.

She looked up at me and innocently asked, "Do you have any kids?"

"No kids."

"Are you married?" Leelee asked.

With an uneasy feeling, I answered, "No, I'm not married, I'm recently divorced." Saying that made me feel like the pink elephant in the room, although the shame I felt regarding this was nothing compared to the demons they were wrestling with.

Vicky, a sweet, innocent-looking young woman with blonde shoulder length hair and crystal blue eyes, seemed to sense my awkwardness as she sat rocking quietly in the rocking chair across from me. She had a "girl-next-door" look and a softer exterior than the rest of the girls.

"I think you will really enjoy it here," Vicky assured me.

As I smiled at Vicky, I was relieved to see Wendy returning with our pizza in hand.

In her cheerful manner, she announced to the girls, "Before we eat, ladies, let us bow our heads with thanks."

I bowed my head, fighting the urge to glance up to see if the girls were actually bowing their heads as well but, from the corner of my eye; I saw them respectively give thanks for their pizza.

****

The next few weeks the House of Love gave me a reason to get out of bed. I no longer felt absorbed with depression and the days seemed to go by faster. The girls started to loosen up to me, and I started to feel more comfortable around them. Wendy felt I was getting used to the girls and their schedule, and she no longer felt the need to accompany me in the house at night.

My first night flying solo, I decided that the girls and I should make brownies.

Leelee begged, "Can I crack the eggs?"

"The eggs are yours for the cracking."

Keisha stood next to Vicky and said, "All I want to do is lick the batter."

"I think we can all partake in that," Amy remarked.

Vicky stirred the batter, poured it into the pan, and put it in the oven. "I am starving. I will probably be able to eat the whole pan."

Keisha replied, "I bet! You're eating for two now, girl!"

Before I could even process what I heard, we were interrupted by a loud knock. As I opened the door, a tall man with dark brown hair, chiseled arms, and a friendly smile stood before me.

Keisha yelled over to him, "Hey, it's Detective McDermott. You must have smelled the brownies."

"Did you ladies bake them just for me?" he asked.

"Of course!" Keisha replied.

"Hi. I'm Detective Eric McDermott. You must be the new girl here," he remarked as he extended his hand to me.

"Hi, I'm Shawnsy," I said, returning his strong handshake.

Lowering his voice, he said, "I am on the task force on human trafficking. I have gotten to know each of these girls a little. I came here tonight to check on Leelee."

"Come on in and have a seat," I said, somewhat confused.

Detective McDermott walked casually to the kitchenette, being familiar with the surroundings, as Leelee followed him. The rest of the girls went to the living room to hang out and watch television while waiting for the brownies to bake, not fazed at all by his appearance.

The oven timer buzzed and I asked as I put on my oven mitts, "Would you like a brownie and a cup of coffee?"

"Sure, I can't say no to either."

Leelee sat comfortably across from him as I let the brownies cool and prepared him a fresh cup of coffee. Detective McDermott stared intently at Leelee and asked, "How are you feeling about next week?"

"I guess all right," Leelee answered, looking down and avoiding any eye contact with him.

Detective McDermott moved his body forward, capturing Leelee's attention.

"You know we can't do this without you. You are the key to putting them away. I will be right there; you have nothing to be afraid of."

The coffee finished percolating and as I walked over to him, I could feel his big brown eyes studying me as I poured his coffee. "Here you go, and here's some cream and sugar."

He gave me a warm smile and thanked me.

Leelee sat looking defeated.

"I think I'm gonna go chill out while the brownies are cooling," she said as if to avoid a confrontation.

While preparing his coffee, he said to Leelee, "Remember Leelee, you have nothing to worry about. I am here for you."

"I know," she said softly, leaving the table.

The detective slowly sipped his coffee and confided to me, "I don't know if you have been briefed yet but Leelee will be testifying at her offenders' trial next week. We really need her testimony to go well. We want to put away the bastards who harmed her, and probably countless others."

"I didn't know anything about this," I said, wondering why Wendy, Alma or any of the girls hadn't mentioned this along with Vicky's pregnancy.

I thought: *Alma did ask me to stop by earlier tomorrow to meet with her; maybe it could be regarding this.*

Suddenly, his cell phone rang. "I have to run," he said, jumping off the seat.

"Oh, but you didn't get to have a brownie."

"I think I'll have to take a rain check. It was great meeting you Shawney."

"It's Shawnsy."

"Pretty name, I'll see you soon."

As he made his way to the door, he shouted, "Bye, ladies. Be good to Miss Shawnsy."

I felt my stomach flutter as he walked out the door.

The girls gathered in the kitchenette to get their warm brownies. The girls were like a little makeshift family; everyone helped out without any guidance. Vicky cut each of the girls a brownie while Leelee poured glasses of milk. We all sat around the dining room table.

"Leelee, did Detective McDermott talk to you about your trial next week?" Keisha asked.

"You always in everyone's Kool-Aid, Keisha," Amy said.

"Huh?" I asked, totally confused.

Amy explained, "If Keisha doesn't have her nose in a book, she has it in somebody else's business."

Keisha responded, "Most of us would love to see our pimps put away, but you, Amy, I'm not so sure. I think you are still in love with your pimp."

"Shut the fuck up, Keisha!" Amy yelled.

Leelee stood up with her hands covering her face, as if trying to conceal her pain, "I can't listen to this anymore. I'm going to my room."

Stunned by Leelee's emotional announcement, everyone remained quiet. Vicky, with her motherly nature, started picking up the plates and putting the milk away. Amy and Keisha retreated to the living room as if nothing had happened.

I followed them out and questioned both of them.

"What is all this about?"

"Why don't you tell her?" Keisha sneered.

"Darius, the man I was with before I came here," Amy started to say.

"Your pimp," Keisha interrupted her.

"Darius wants me to come home."

Vicky returned from the kitchen, and in her matronly way asked, "Amy, I thought this was your home now?"

"No, this is just a place for me to get my shit together. It's not my home."

Keisha shook her head and said, "It doesn't seem like you got your shit together either."

Amy just sat there with a look as if she had given up, knowing there was no winning with Keisha.

Chapter 3

It was a bright sunny day, with a nippy coolness to the air, a reminder that a northeast winter would soon be approaching.

As I made my way across the campus, I saw Alma. "I was just going to look for you," I said, glad that she had saved me the trouble.

"Oh good, do you mind if we walk and talk?" she asked as she continued to walk at a fast speed. "How are things coming along at the House of Love?"

"Great," I said, trying my best to keep up with her.

"I have heard that the girls have taken a liking to you. That's very important. I want to discuss some matters with you. Leelee will be having a tough week next week. She is going to have to testify in court."

I caught my breath and slowed my pace, hoping Alma would follow, "I found out through Detective McDermott. He stopped by and gave me the heads-up about it," I said, still wanting more information.

Continuing at her own fast pace, she responded, "Oh, you met the great Detective McDermott. He's a godsend for getting these animals off the streets. Between him and the District Attorney, and with Leelee's testimony, I think we should have a strong case. Shawnsy, would you mind going to court with them next week? Family is not in the picture and she could use some female support. Wendy will be very busy holding down the rest of the fort."

"Absolutely," I answered, without question. "I wouldn't mind at all."

"And if you haven't heard already, Vicky is pregnant. We don't know what her decision will be regarding this, but we at St. Agnes' Place pray that she will make a wise decision considering the child's welfare."

"Nobody officially told me, but I can't believe it. Vicky is just a child herself," I said.

"Yes, they all are like kittens that have had nine lives. If you would like some extra hours, Vicky could use someone at her side as well as she goes through her pregnancy. If you wouldn't mind taking her to her appointments and helping her with anything she may need, it would be greatly appreciated. Vicky does come from a wonderful family, but they are quite a distance away, and it does seem like she is bonding quite well with you from what I have heard."

"Thank you. Vicky really is a very sweet girl and I don't mind helping out in any way I can. But, I do have one concern. There has been talk that Amy has been in contact with a past boyfriend or pimp, I'm not quite sure which it is."

"Miss Stevens we do our very best to lead the girls on the proper path, but where they choose to go is ultimately up to them. Believe it or not, it usually takes several times for many of the girls to leave the streets for good. We can only provide a road map for them. But you should be very proud of yourself. You are doing a great job."

"Thank you, Alma." Hearing that any of the girls would even consider going back to that life put an ache in my heart, but hearing the words "great job" made me feel wonderful inside.

****

The next few days, I sat by Leelee's side as she met with attorneys and law clerks, making sure all the finishing touches were done on her case. So much was riding on Leelee's testimony I could see it taking its toll on her. I understood her pain. I knew that pain is pain no matter how intense the situation is that caused it. Leelee was not eating and retreated to her room more often, barely interacting with the other girls. The only time I saw her come alive was at night when the other girls were getting ready for bed. She would come down and we would sit on the couch and look through magazines I brought in. We would share comments on the crazy outfits the celebrities were wearing or who was dating whom in Hollywood. On the nights *Animal Rescue* was on, we would both watch with sadness and disbelief at what was happening to the animals, but waited with anticipation for their rescue and new homes. Although the shows were heartbreaking, I think Leelee identified with the neglected animals. Other than our special times together at night, I thought Leelee seemed to be just going through the motions.

It was finally the day of the trial. I arrived early to pick Leelee up. I could feel her nervous energy pass through me.

"How are you feeling?" I asked her.

"Good. I just want to get this over with."

"You are going to do great," Vicky said, hugging her tight.

"Tell them everything. Give them what they deserve," Keisha said, hugging her.

"You'll be all right," Amy said, high-fiving her.

"You will be fine, Leelee," I assured her.

We were to meet Detective McDermott and District Attorney John Rossi an hour early to make sure everything started smoothly.

I grabbed Leelee's hand. "God is with you Leelee, and Detective McDermott and I will be right there as well."

Leelee looked very mature that day. She wore gray slacks and a white turtleneck, a much different look than the low cut jeans and hoodie I was used to seeing her in. Detective McDermott and the District Attorney were anxiously waiting outside the courtroom for us.

"You are going to do great today," Detective McDermott said affectionately.

Leelee just nodded her head.

The District Attorney, John Rossi, asked as if he were preparing for war, "Do you have any other questions, Leelee?"

"No," Leelee responded.

I gave her a kiss on her forehead. "You're going to do great, Leelee."

When Leelee approached the bench, she looked so young and innocent. To see someone suffer so much at such a young age seemed so unfair. Leelee stared straight ahead, looking past all the faces in the courtroom. It was obvious she was in complete control. The District Attorney asked her to explain the relationship between her and Derrick "Chili" Johnson. As Leelee flashed back to the events, I felt like I was a bystander in a real life horror film.

Leelee spoke softly and slowly, "I was twelve years old and I lived with my mom and her new boyfriend. My mom and I weren't getting along, and her new boyfriend hated me, and I hated him. My mom and her boyfriend were always fighting about money or how lazy he was, so I'd be running the streets. That's where I met Chili. He was older, around eighteen or nineteen years old. He liked me and he kept telling me how beautiful I was. Chili was good to me at first. He took me to eat and he bought me some real nice clothes. I started staying over at his place. My mom didn't care. She was drunk half the time, and she had her hands full with her new boyfriend. When I was at Chili's, she didn't have to deal with me. It was the summertime and she was used to me being out all night anyway.

"One night Chili said to me, 'I'm gonna have some friends over tonight.' I said, 'That's cool.' Then he asked me, 'You'll do anything for me, right girl?' Chili be taking care of me so I told him, 'Chili, you know that.' I didn't know what he was talking about and I didn't ask. That night we drank some beer and smoked some weed. Later some men arrived. I'd never seen them before with Chili. Chili said, 'You gonna do me right.' I didn't know what he was talking about."

I sat there holding my face. I could feel the warm tears and mascara running down my face as I listened to Leelee.

"The rest of the night, I just lay there numb as different men came and left Chili's dark bedroom. They did whatever they wanted to me."

Leelee began to break down as the tears continued to stream down her face. "I didn't leave that night, I couldn't get myself out of bed I felt so ashamed."

"In the morning, Chili brought me in orange juice and some doughnuts. Chili said, 'I did good and I needed to be rewarded.'

"That afternoon Chili got me out of bed and took me shopping at the mall.

"I didn't think about if this was going to happen again, but Chili kept saying, 'You're my girl.' The next night began as a repeat of the first. I told Chili I wasn't comfortable, and didn't like it. He just said, 'Bitch, I don't care what you like or don't like because you're mine now. I've been taking care of your sorry ass, and you're gonna pay me back.'

"Then he pulled my hair and slammed my body against the wall.

"I don't even remember how many men came or what they looked like. All I heard was the loud blare of Chili's boom box playing in the background.

"After the second night, Chili wouldn't let me leave his apartment. If he went anywhere, he had his homeboy, "King" watch me and have his way with me.

"I knew my mom didn't even know where Chili lived, and my biggest fear was that she thought I just took off with him. I was held captive. If Chili wasn't beating me with his fists, he made sure I knew the presence of his gun.

"The nights ran together. I wanted to die, yet I feared Chili would kill me if I tried to leave. Nothing made sense. I felt I wasn't even present in my own body."

The courtroom was in a stunned silence as the District Attorney interrupted by asking, "As horrific as the events that occurred to you, did Mr. Johnson's torment escalate to a higher level?"

Leelee continued trying desperately to hold her composure, "One night some grandfatherly looking guy came over, and Chili said, 'We gonna pretend it's Halloween.' I was real nervous but I didn't say anything. I was too scared. The old man said, 'Put on this school-girl outfit and put your hair in pigtails. You're gonna be my little girl.' Then he told me to pose while he took some pictures."

There was an awkward silence throughout the courtroom as the District Attorney asked, "Did anything else occur that night, Leelee?"

Leelee started to lose control and in a loud voice answered, "The old man raped me!"

The District Attorney continued by asking, "What was Mr. Johnson doing while this was going on?"

Leelee, overwhelmed with emotion, answered, "Chili just stood there. He just stood there taping it."

There was an uncomfortable silence throughout the courtroom. I felt sick to my stomach hearing her story. I could see the smug expression of the monster sitting nonchalantly across from Leelee. I felt like a mother hen, wanting to lunge at him and hurt him in any physical way I could. Sadly, neither Leelee's mother nor any other family member was present.

The District Attorney ended the questioning by saying, "It was by sheer luck that Leelee was even saved. A few months later, the police arrived for a petty warrant that was issued for Derrick "Chili" Johnson and in his apartment the officers found the battered, scared, and underage Leelee."

****

Leelee, Detective McDermott and I returned back to the house later that afternoon. I was glad the house was empty while the girls were attending their classes and treatments. We were all at a loss for words.

"Leelee, would you like me to go to the dining hall and get you something to eat?"

"No, I just want to go lay down," Leelee answered despondently.

Detective McDermott stood by her side and said, "You did great today, and if you need anything, I am here for you."

"I am going to walk her upstairs," I said.

"I'm going to be relaxing right here. I am in no mood to do anything else."

I followed Leelee up to her bedroom. I sat beside her while she lay in bed.

"I hate them. I hate myself," she said with tears in her eyes.

"Leelee, what they did to you was wrong. Don't ever hate yourself. You are a strong young woman." I embraced her as she continued facing the wall.

I rubbed her shoulders and arms, noticing the fresh cuts escalating up her arms. Leelee fell asleep, and I softly wrapped the comforter over her.

I quietly went back downstairs and was surprised to see that Detective McDermott was still there.

"Leelee fell asleep. Can I get you something to drink, Detective McDermott?"

"Shawnsy, you can call me Eric."

I didn't know what to say.

"I could sure use a beer," Eric said with a smile.

"Me, too," I said, wishing I really had one. "Would a glass of apple juice do?"

"Sounds good, and if the jury finds them guilty we should go celebrate; with a beer, of course," Eric suggested.

"It sure sounds good to me!"

Chapter 4

I was actually relieved to have a weekend off. Walking over the mounds of clothing that cluttered my laundry room was starting to get frustrating. The refrigerator needed cleaning and I couldn't remember the last time I went grocery shopping. Being so caught up in the girls' lives, I had forgotten to take care of the everyday essentials in mine. The phone rang. I thought: *another call from my mother.*

"Hello, Shawnsy. It's Eric."

"Hi, is everything all right?"

"Yeah, everything is great. I was wondering if you had any plans for tonight?"

I was taken aback and said, "No, what's going on?"

"The police department sponsors a holiday light show in Washington Park. I thought we could go look at the pretty lights, and maybe go get a cup of coffee or a beer afterwards."

"That sounds nice," I said, wondering if this was actually a date.

"Great. I will pick you up at six."

"Wait, let me tell you how to get here," I said suddenly.

"Shawnsy, you forgot I'm a detective. I'll see you at six."

I thought: *A date; what would Jon think? Wait, why do I care? He's with a girl who stills wears a retainer!*

I looked at myself in the mirror. I had actually lost a few pounds since the divorce and there were no grays yet in my dirty blonde hair. I was actually starting to feel good about myself, although I was a little nervous. I hadn't been on a date since I was nineteen years old, and that had been with Jon.

At 6:00, Eric arrived in a little beat-up Volkswagen.

"Oh, I thought I would be driving in a cop car today," I said as I greeted him at the door.

"No, not tonight, but I do have the gun, the badge, and even handcuffs," he said with a laugh.

"That's good to know."

"You have a beautiful home," Eric said, glancing around.

"Why, thank you," I said, as I grabbed my purse.

Like a perfect gentleman, he opened the car door for me.

"Oh, you smell nice," Eric said.

"Thanks," I said, looking up at him.

"You know, I'm like a big kid during this time of the year. I know Christmas is on its way when it's time for the holiday light show," he said cheerfully.

I loved his enthusiasm, even though I always thought it was the most stressful time of the year. During this time, Jon needed accountability more than ever for every dime I spent.

"Do you have any kids?" I asked, without much thought.

"No, but I love kids. I was married for a short time and she had kids from her previous marriage. I loved her kids, but when the marriage went south, so did the relationship with the kids. I never missed her, but I still think about the kids."

"What about you? Kids didn't fit the plan?" he asked.

"No it wasn't that. I love kids, but I can't have them. I guess it's not in the cards."

"You never know, Shawnsy, what life may bring."

We drove into the park. It was illuminated with colored lights. Eric cranked the Christmas music on the radio. "Dominic the Donkey" came on, and with child-like enthusiasm, Eric sang along while pointing to the various Christmas displays.

As we exited the park, Eric asked, "Are you hungry?"

"Yeah, a little bit."

"Would you like to go to one of my favorite places, and it's not Dunkin Donuts?"

"Sure," I said, enjoying the ride.

We arrived at a quaint diner decorated with festive holiday lights and wreaths. An older waitress with a strong Greek accent greeted Eric with a hug.

"It's so good to see you again. It's been a long time," she said in accented English.

"It's good to see you too, Lainie. Do you have your wonderful chicken pot pies tonight?"

"We do. We have them just for you. And, who is this beautiful lady?"

"This beautiful lady is my friend Shawnsy," he said, putting his arm around me.

"Hello," I said, surprised that he wrapped his arm around me.

"Come have a seat," she said leading us to a booth.

I looked over the menu and Eric convinced me to order the chicken pot pie, something I hadn't had since I was kid.

"Shawnsy, how did you come to get such a beautiful and distinct name?"

"If you really want to know, the story is my parents could not agree on what to name me, and when they took my older sister Gwen to visit her new sissy in the hospital, she just called me Shawnsy, and the name stuck."

"Interesting," he said with a flirty smile, his eyebrows raised. "You have only one sister?"

"Just a sister, she is about two years older than me and lives with her husband in California. What about you?"

"I have two older brothers."

"Oh, so you're the baby."

"Yep, I was the wild little guy they all had to chase after."

"Now they have a superhero in the family. Their wild little brother grew up and became a detective."

"I like to think of myself as the ultimate crime fighter," he said with a slight chuckle.

"Your family must be very proud of you."

"I hope. We are a proud Irish family, and we all happen to work within the police department. My father was a cop, and my older brother is a state trooper. My other brother is also a cop, and he lives in Long Island with his wife and kids."

"You definitely have a crime fighting family. I take it your dad is retired?"

"Pops is retired, but he lives through my work, and my mom passed away about five years ago. She always stayed home and took care of all of us. How about your parents?"

"My mom is a retired secretary, and my dad died about ten years ago from lung cancer."

"I'm sorry to hear that."

"My sister Gwen and her husband actually live in Silicon Valley and are the big corporate types," I sighed.

"I'm sorry to hear that too."

Our chicken pot pies arrived, and I felt giddy sitting there. I wiped my face constantly, making sure there was no gravy on it.

"Are you up for dessert?" Eric asked.

"I don't think I could eat a whole dessert."

"They have the best apple crisp around. How 'bout we split it?"

"I guess I can't refuse."

Eric signaled the waitress. "We will have two coffees, Lainie, and we are going to split your fabulous apple crisp."

"I'll bring it right out to you," she said with a gleaming smile.

The dessert came with two forks. We both let out a nervous giggle.

"Dig in, but no stealing all the crunchies on top," he kidded, pointing with his fork to the top of the apple crisp.

I dug my fork into the melted whip cream and scooped up some crunchies. "But that's usually the best part!" I said smiling at him.

****

I couldn't believe I had just gone out on a date, and he was actually cute and nice. I didn't remember feeling this much excitement in such a long time. I felt like I was having a junior-high crush. Maybe I shouldn't feel this happy. Could this be just a "get-together" to him? I couldn't wait to see Eric again. I didn't think I would ever be able to fall asleep.

Chapter 5

It was time to go back to work. I was starting to miss the girls already, even though I had only been away for a couple of days. I arrived and heard rap music blaring. Vicky was rocking in her favorite chair and Keisha was lying on the floor, surrounded by her books while Amy entertained them with her sexy moves.

"Nice dance moves, Amy," I commented as I walked through the living room.

"Don't encourage her, Shawnsy. Plus, this pimpin' music encourages everything we are all fighting against. I wrote a whole paper on it for my Social Issues class and I even got an A on it," Keisha said.

"Why don't you go get it and hang it on the fridge?" Amy asked sarcastically.

"I just might do that!"

"Keisha, didn't you have the biggest gangsta-rap collection when you first came here?" Amy asked, as she continued to dance.

Keisha continued writing, pretending to ignore Amy. I turned off their CD player.

"Come on, Shawnsy, you don't like this kind of music?" Amy asked.

"No, I agree with Keisha on this one."

"Me, too, Shawnsy," Vicky added.

"Are you girls all set to go to the dining hall?"

"Yeah, I'm starving," Keisha said.

"Where's Leelee?" I asked.

"She's in the bathroom. She's been in there for quite awhile. If it's not Vicky spending all her time in there, it's Leelee," Keisha remarked.

"I have good reason; I happen to be with child," Vicky smiled, patting her stomach.

"Why don't you girls go ahead," I said, thinking I could use some private time with Leelee to talk with her and see how she was feeling.

After the girls left, I gently knocked on the door. "Leelee, are you all right in there?"

There was no response. I knocked hesitantly one more time. I started to feel uneasy.

"Leelee, are you all right?" I asked nervously.

Leelee did not respond.

I pushed on the door, and it opened. I felt sheer panic. I walked in, feeling as if I were walking on broken glass. I gasped when I saw Leelee lying in the tub with her arms extended with blood dripping into the half-filled bathtub. I grabbed Leelee's limp body.

"No, Leelee. No! Oh my God, please help her! Please help her!" I screamed.

I took my cell phone out of my pocket and dialed 911.

The paramedics came within minutes and Leelee was pronounced dead at the scene.

****

Moments later, Eric arrived. He held my head to his chest. I just cried as he stroked my hair. Thoughts of Leelee and I together flashed through my mind. We had developed such a close bond before the trial. I remember sitting in the courtroom wishing I could take the stand for her. I realized her tough exterior was a protective wall she had built to keep anyone from harming her. Unfortunately, it kept many from getting close. I was fortunate that Leelee had allowed me into her heart. I had loved our late night talks on the couch. We had talked about movies, men and our favorite things. Leelee and I had shared a love for the movie *The Wizard of Oz*. We both loved Glinda and thought she was too beautiful to exist in real life, and the flying monkeys freaked both of us out. I think Leelee had wished Oz was a real place where she could go to escape all her pain. How I wish I could have waved a magic wand and sent her there.

Leelee had trusted me enough to share her dreams with me. She often spoke about her love of animals, even though she never actually had one. We had both agreed horses were the most beautiful animal. I had even promised her that during the spring I would take her horseback riding. I had confessed to Leelee how I was still struggling with forgiveness toward my ex-husband Jon, and whether or not the right thing was to take him back if he came running. Leelee's only advice to me was to stay away from "Johns." I didn't catch on to it at first, but then we both laughed.

I saw a colorful butterfly emerge from this dark young girl. I saw a child who needed to be loved, rather than a dark haired, dark-skinned ghetto-tough Latina, trying to act bigger than her five-foot stature. Leelee was a beauty that needed nurturing and a fresh start. But, most of all, she had needed to feel that she was truly loved, and I had loved her.

Alma arrived, and it was obvious she was trying hard to keep it together.

She gave me a hard hug. "I am so sorry, Shawnsy. I am going to go tell the girls now."

"Let me go with you!" I pleaded.

"You get yourself together and I'll bring them back in a few hours. Plus, everything should be cleaned up by then."

I sat there, unable to move. Eric continued stroking my hair as tears streamed down my face.

After a few minutes, he said, "I'll be right back."

He slowly exited the porch and let the other staff and on-lookers know about Leelee's death.

****

Hours later, Alma arrived with Keisha, Amy and Vicky. They all looked distraught and shocked.

"I am so sorry, girls," I said, trying hard to fight back the tears.

Vicky came over and hugged me. It was a long hug. Neither one of us wanted to let go.

All of us went into the house and gathered around the living room.

"Alma, I'm going to stay over for the night if that's all right?" I asked.

"That's fine." Alma tried noticeably hard to maintain her authoritative persona, and fighting back tears said, "Girls, listen to me. Look at me! What Leelee did was wrong. I know she was hurting and obviously in deep pain. But she let them win. God always forgives you, please get over any shame you may feel. All of you are so beautiful and full of so much promise."

Keisha went over and hugged Alma. We all just sat around in silence.

****

Alma called Wendy and informed her of what happened. It was her day off and although she was visiting her family out of town, she said she would be there as soon as possible. When she arrived, we were all in a quiet state of shock and disbelief. Wendy went to each one of us and gave us a sympathetic hug.

"Is there anything I can do?" she asked. We all just shook our heads.

"I can't believe what she did!" Amy said.

"I feel terrible. We should have realized how upset she had been lately," Vicky said tearfully.

With strong conviction, Wendy said, "Now listen, you girls. You can't blame yourselves for what happened. No one can."

We all barely spoke the rest of the evening. Eric asked repeatedly if there was anything he could do. After Alma and Wendy left, the girls brought their pillows and blankets to the living room and set up a make-shift camp on the floor.

"I'm going to be heading out, ladies," Eric said as he hugged each of them.

I followed him out to the front porch.

"Are you going to be all right tonight?"

"I'll be fine," I said, barely able to get the words out.

"I will check on all of you tomorrow morning," he said as he slowly kissed my forehead.

Chapter 6

The news of Leelee's death hit everyone hard. The girls were spending extra time in therapy and meeting with a grief counselor. I also met with the grief counselor twice, which helped put to rest any doubts that I had about not being there enough for Leelee. I realized what I knew all along in my heart was that Leelee's death should be mourned, but her decision to end her life was nothing that we should feel guilty about.

Eric surprised us and arrived at the house with boxes of Christmas decorations.

"I thought this would cheer everyone up," he said enthusiastically.

"You are so thoughtful, and you really are a big kid during this time of the year," I said.

"I saw what they had hung up last year. This place looked like Doomesville."

As I was going through the boxes of ornaments, Eric bent down next to me and smiled. I loved looking at his dimples whenever he smiled. He put his hand on my knees and asked, "How are you doing?"

"I'm hanging in there," I said.

We were suddenly interrupted by Keisha's loud entrance.

"Wow, what do we have here?" she asked.

"We are going to make this place into a real winter wonderland," Eric announced.

Vicky and Amy walked down from their rooms.

"Girls, it's time to decorate," Eric informed them.

"Woohoo," Amy said.

"I love to decorate," Vicky said enthusiastically, looking into the boxes.

"Amy, plug in your CD player and put in one of those Christmas CDs I put on the table."

"Eric, you didn't forget a thing," I said.

"I was worried about all of you; plus, it's Christmas."

"You're so kind! I love this artificial Charlie Brown tree," Keisha said, laughing while pulling it clumsily out of the box.

"Detective McDermott, don't you have any modern Christmas CDs instead of this old stuff?" Amy asked.

"This is real Christmas music. Nothing like Nat King Cole or Bing Crosby to get you in the spirit!" Eric said.

Amy put in the CD, and Bing Crosby's "Chestnuts Roasting on an Open Fire" echoed through the house.

"Amy, let's see you dance to this," Keisha said.

Amy shook her head and laughed.

It was funny to watch Vicky ostentatiously decorate the tiny tree, while Amy and Keisha casually hung the decorations.

"Princess, what are you doing when you leave here?" Eric whispered, as we went through a box of decorations.

"I have no plans," I whispered back.

Eric said, quietly and animatedly looking around as if to see if the coast was clear, "How about you come over to my place and we can hang out and watch a movie."

"Sounds good to me," I said, whispering and trying to hold back my laughter at how silly he was acting.

I loved spending time with him. His carefree, goofy attitude made me forget everything that had been going on.

"Jingle Bell Rock" played, and Eric and the girls sang as if in an off-key choir. He was right—this was exactly what we all needed. Our little House of Love was starting to get its spirit back.

****

I arrived at his place later that night, and Eric greeted me at the door with a huge grin, "And how was your night?"

I was a little bit startled at first. Behind him stood a huge Rottweiler that looked as if it could eat me for breakfast.

"It was great, thank you. Does he bite?" I asked nervously.

"Come on in, she's a pussy cat," he said, petting the huge dog.

I followed Eric in, and his dog stood right by his side.

"This is Angus Beef, and she's a sweetheart."

"Nice name."

"Angie, it's time to go to your corner."

The large dog obediently walked over to the corner of the living room. A loud thud was heard as she dropped to the floor with her head down.

"Sit down, relax. Can I get you something to drink? I have beer, wine, soda, water...."

"Water is fine," I said looking around his apartment. It was a true bachelor pad: Yankees memorabilia hung on the walls, and from the living room, a full view of scattered laundry could be seen from his open bedroom door. Scattered about the end tables were family pictures. I got up and looked at the pictures, while Angus Beef looked up at me, staying obediently in her position.

On one of the tables was a picture of Eric with his mother as he was being sworn into the police department. "I like this picture of you and your mother."

"Thank you," he yelled from the kitchen.

"And these kids are adorable," I said, looking at a typical family portrait of a brother and sister smiling on command.

"Those are my niece and nephew," Eric said as he returned with a bottle of Heineken and a glass of water for me. We sat a comfortable distance apart from each other.

"How are you like this?" I asked.

"What do you mean?"

"You deal with such terrible things. You see evil everyday and yet you are so easy-going, and so happy."

"It comes with time. Everyone sees evil everyday. I may see the monsters, but I know at the end of the day I worked hard to make a difference in this world. Not everyone can say that when they come home from work each day," Eric answered.

"Shawnsy, tell me. How's your life going?" Eric asked as he opened his beer.

"Good for being recently divorced, starting a new job and witnessing the aftermath of a suicide."

"Wow, you are one busy lady. I am so sorry you had to go through what you did. The girls were so lucky to have you there. And, if you don't mind me asking, was it a messy divorce?"

"No, it wasn't messy. He was very fair. It was just one big surprise, and I didn't see it coming. What about your short-lived marriage? Was your divorce messy?" I asked.

"The divorce wasn't messy, the whole marriage was messy." Eric chuckled. "I think that both of us were just anxious to settle down. It was a big mistake. Would you like to try settling down again someday?"

"I haven't really given it much thought since Jon and I divorced. But I would be open to it. I can't have the kids, but I wouldn't mind the whole white picket fence thing."

"That's a good thing," he said, smiling at me. "So, Miss Shawnsy, what kind of movies do you like?"

"I actually like all types of movies."

"We can either order one, or we can go through my vast assortment."

"I'll let you surprise me," I said.

"How about something with Will Ferrell? We can't go wrong with him. He's a classic."

"Sounds good to me."

Eric put in the movie, and the personal space between us slowly began to get smaller.

****

As I was about to leave, Eric stopped me, looked deeply into my eyes and said, "I had a really nice time tonight."

"Me, too," I said.

"I need to know, do you like Will Ferrell?"

"Oh, yeah, I like Will Ferrell."

Eric wrapped my scarf around me and asked, "Do you like me, Shawnsy?"

I looked into his piercing dark eyes; his big arms were still holding my scarf. "Yes, I like you, Eric."

Eric gently kissed my forehead and said, "Thank you for coming over."

I looked up at him and softly smiled.

As I walked down the driveway, I heard Eric shout, "Watch out!"

As I turned around to look at him, he threw a snowball at me. I grabbed some snow, made a snowball, and threw it at him.

A war began between us, as he came farther down the driveway with just his t-shirt on.

Eric came closer to me and, whether it was by accident or by design, he threw me back completely into the snow. "You're a beautiful woman, Shawnsy." His cold hand feathered my hair, and his hard body laid into mine.

"So what does Shawnsy say?"

"What?" I asked, somewhat confused.

"Does Shawnsy want to be my girl?"

"Yes, she does!"

Eric laid his soft lips on mine and we kissed.

Chapter 7

Things were looking up in the house. Eric stopped in to announce that Leelee's offenders were found guilty. The girls showed mixed emotions. The verdict seemed to open up old wounds from which they were desperately trying to heal from.

As Vicky rocked in her chair, she meekly said, "I never had the satisfaction of seeing the people who harmed me be put to justice. I guess it's just as well. Look what it did to Leelee."

"They were put away. Fortunately, they plea-bargained and you didn't have to testify," Eric explained.

"I don't think I could have ever done what Leelee did. It would have killed me too. They were just so awful!"

"What exactly did they do to you, Vicky, if you don't mind talking about it?" I asked.

"I don't mind acknowledging what they did to me because it helps me put it into perspective. My friend and I were vulnerable teenagers with dreams of someday becoming models. Looking back I realize how naïve we both were," Vicky said shaking her head while continuing to rock in her chair.

"We were all young and naïve," Keisha said.

"But they were so convincing. They posed as a husband and wife who owned a modeling agency. They offered to take pictures of us. If things went well, we could sign up with them and possibly have our faces in magazines. My friend and I left the mall with them. We should have known better. Both of our parents were against the modeling thing. They were so strict. I wasn't even allowed to wear a two-piece bathing suit. We both agreed we would just go with them and see what would happen. I can't believe I'm still alive today to talk about it. I guess they didn't break me completely.

"They said we needed to go to their studio near the mall, and that it would only take a half-hour for the pictures. The woman seemed real nice, and we both trusted her. Their studio was actually a hotel room that they rented by the week. Things started to get real creepy, and we were scared. They forced us to pose in dirty ways, while they took pictures of us. They told us they were going to post the pictures on-line. My friend started to freak out. I was in shock the whole time. The man told the woman to take her back to the mall. My friend was told if she said anything, they would kill me. I was told to stay. Thankfully, when my friend got home, she told her parents everything. They called my parents, who contacted the police. The police got a good description from my friend, but, unfortunately, they moved me to another hotel. From what I was told, they travel from state to state trafficking girls like me.

"The next two and a half weeks, which seemed like forever, was a nightmare. They did with me whatever they wanted. So many men responded to their ad, and none of them ever questioned my age. I zoned out the whole time. I realized, through therapy, that zoning out had become my defense mechanism. Thank God I was finally rescued! The police investigated all the local online ads for escorts, and that's how they found me. It was a miracle because I remember them talking about leaving in a few days for a new town.

"When I returned home, all of my family and friends treated me differently. I still felt that I had disappointed all of them. Although they constantly reassured me, things just didn't feel the same way they did before everything happened to me. So I started to rebel. I started to experiment with drugs, and I took off with some older jerk I barely knew. I called my parents the night I took off with him. I was scared, pregnant and a total mess. My parents rescued me, but instead of sending me home, they sent me here. I'm glad they did. It's just now I have a fear of going back home."

I got up and hugged Vicky. "I am so sorry this happened to you."

She didn't say anything, but just hugged me back.

"You're lucky you have a family to go home to," Keisha said.

"I do realize that, but I feel so guilty for everything I put them through. My mother was going through breast cancer. She's in remission now. It was the last thing they needed. It destroyed all of us."

Keisha confessed, "I still struggle with guilt too, Vicky. But I guess getting over it is the only way we are ever going to heal. For the longest time not only did I feel dirty, but I was also treated like a criminal. When my cousin and her boyfriend were finally held accountable for what they did to me, I felt relieved but I knew deep inside that a lot of damage was done to me."

"It don't even matter though that they put your cousin and her man away 'cause they always get out, and they all be up to their same old tricks," Amy said.

"And they got bitches like you waiting for them at their doorstep," Keisha answered.

"Who the fuck do you think you are talking to?" Amy asked as she angrily walked over to Keisha and gave her a right hook. Keisha returned the punch.

I couldn't even speak. Thankfully, Eric was there to separate them. I wouldn't have had the strength to pull them apart.

"Ladies, this is no way to act!" Eric said with his arms stretched out separating the two of them.

Vicky and I just sat there, speechless.

Amy shouted, "I am sick of her sly little comments!"

"Well, I'm sick of your stupidity!" Keisha shouted back.

"That's enough! I am so disappointed in the two of you. Now go get ready for dinner!" I exclaimed.

I could tell they were surprised at the angry tone I used, and I knew they did not like hearing how they had disappointed me. Keisha and Amy both left the room speechless.

"I am going to go use the bathroom," Vicky announced.

"I'm glad you're my calm one, Vicky." I smiled over at her.

"I'm going to be heading out. Vicky, please help Shawnsy man the fort," Eric yelled to her.

"Sure," Vicky said as she left the room.

"Are we seeing each other later?" Eric asked, as if nothing had just taken place.

"Sure. I could use a break," I said, feeling worn out.

"And, Shawnsy, please don't let them kill each other in the meantime."

"I'll try my best. See you tonight."

Eric quickly gave me a kiss on the lips before he made his way out the door.

Eric and I kept our relationship a secret, although I guessed the girls suspected there was something going on between us.

****

The girls were ready to head over to the dining hall. Keisha and Amy acted as if nothing had just happened, and there were no bruises to serve as a reminder.

While at the dining hall, Alma came over to me. "Hello, ladies. Shawnsy, can I speak to you for a moment?"

"Sure," I said, leaving the table. I followed Alma to an empty table.

"How is everything going?" Alma asked.

"Good," I said, not wanting to mention the brawl that had just taken place.

In a pleasant tone, Alma said, "It seems like things are getting back to normal since Leelee's death, and I am glad that her offenders were found guilty."

I agreed. "We are all very happy about that, and the girls and I are coming along fine in light of what happened."

"I want to talk to you about Keisha."

"Is everything all right?"

"Oh, yes, Keisha is excelling in all her classes. She is also progressing quite well in therapy. She is a highly intelligent young woman. I don't believe St. Agnes' is the best place for her anymore."

"What?" I asked, surprised. "Where do you want her to go?"

"I understand we have all fallen in love with Keisha. We want the very best for her. I personally looked into some very good boarding schools that foster high academic achievement. We have some donations that I could approve being used for this. She is ready for this, Shawnsy."

"You're right," I said hesitantly. I knew in my heart that given the opportunity, Keisha would flourish.

Alma spoke with Keisha. As I thought, Keisha was excited about the opportunity to go away to a private school next year.

"I told you all I was a genius," Keisha exclaimed.

"Yes, Dr. Keisha," Amy said.

"Don't you all be surprised if I become one someday," Keisha shot back.

"Keisha, I am so proud of you. I am really proud of all of you. We are truly going to miss you next year, Keisha," I said.

"Speak for yourself," Amy said, as she playfully pushed Keisha on the couch.

"I do love you, Miss Shawnsy," Keisha said as she got up and gave me a hug. "I'm ready to move on. I feel good about myself now," Keisha said with cool confidence.

Vicky said, "You can do anything you want in life, Keisha."

"I truly believe that now. When I was first rescued, I was sent to juvie, and treated like a criminal. I was fourteen years old; those niggas didn't even have the legal right to fuck with me. But when I was sent here, everything changed," Keisha said, sounding relieved.

"Now she is a Little Miss Know It All," Amy said kiddingly to Keisha.

"She does always have her head in a book," Vicky added.

"I owe that to my grandmother. When I was a little girl, I lived with her when my own mom was off running the streets. She read to me everyday. When she died, I was back with my mom and her new man, and I never got read to again," Keisha said.

Vicky said, running toward the bathroom, "I'm going to get sick!"

"See, you are making Vicky sick with all your reading shit," Amy teased Keisha again.

Keisha shot back, "Give me the remote so I don't have to listen to your mouth."

I walked to the bathroom to check on Vicky.

"Vicky, is everything all right?" I asked, knocking on the door.

"I'm fine, you can come in."

She was on her knees, curled over the toilet. I bent down and rubbed her back. "How does it feel to be pregnant?"

"It sucks," she said, wiping the spit from her face.

"I understand. It's no fun getting sick."

"I don't know if it's the baby, or the fact that my parents are coming to visit next week that is making me feel so sick."

"It's nice your parents want to see you."

"Yeah, it's good that they haven't given up on me, not yet anyway."

"Vicky, you are such a sweet girl. I'm sure your parents love you very much."

"I guess," Vicky said, as she splashed water on her face.

Vicky and I returned to the living room, where Amy had control of the remote now.

Keisha was writing away in her notebook.

"What are you writing?" Vicky asked, curling up next to her.

"I'm writing some poetry. You know how they are always saying in counseling about how therapeutic it is for us."

"I'm really not into poetry. It's very confusing to me," Vicky said.

"Keisha, whatever it is you are doing keep it up. You are on the right path," I said, rocking in the chair.

Keisha let out a wise laugh and said, "Shawnsy, if you saw me two years ago, I think you would have been afraid of me."

"Not our sweet Keisha," I said smiling.

"Shawnsy, I didn't trust anyone! I was so used to people using me, I couldn't accept love. Like I was telling you, the only love I knew was from my grandmother. She always believed in me. She made sure I was fed, and got me to school each day. When she died, my world fell apart. My mother didn't know how to take care of me. She couldn't even take care of herself. She always had a different man, and most of them seemed to have more of an interest in me than her. The last man who lived with us abused me, and my mother knew he was abusing me, but the way she looked at it, it was nothing that her own daddy didn't do to her; plus, he was helping her put the food on the table. My cousin Tracey and her boyfriend started coming around, and I always looked up to her. I saw how good she was doing and I wanted to be just like her. My cousin and her boyfriend convinced me to strip. The strip club knew I was underage, and they didn't care. I actually liked it at first. I got a lot of attention because of it. I was buying a lot of stuff. Things changed fast. I became my cousin and her boyfriend's property. They had me staying in their apartment. If I wasn't stripping, they had me turning tricks. They kept everything. I think I went along with them because I felt they actually cared about me. That's how messed up I was. I started becoming my cousin's boyfriend's main girl. I was, like, thirteen years old."

"You were just a baby," I said.

"I realize that now," Keisha said, shaking her head.

"When my cousin seen her boyfriend taking a liking to me, that really pissed her off. They made me feel guilty about everything I had done. I couldn't go back home because it was no better there with my mom's boyfriend, and she probably would have told my cousin to just keep me. My cousin had her eye on me all the time. They made it where I couldn't leave. They had me using drugs and beat me anytime I defied them. Finally, my cousin couldn't take the attention her man, well, "our" man, was giving me, as sick as that sounds. She got pissed, and on her watch, she literally threw me out. I ended up on the streets and landed in juvie, and finally was given the choice to come here."

"Thank God for St. Agnes' Place," Vicky said.

"That's for sure, and the hardest thing I had to do since coming here was learning to forgive my family. My mom and my cousin were supposed to protect me. I still struggle with forgiving them but I know I must in order to move on. This place taught me that what happens in a home is sacred and what it means to have a family. I actually thank God each morning that I am alive, and give the day to Him. I ask Him to take away my anger, and in return, He has given me peace."

Amy cheered, "Amen, sistah!"

Keisha looked over at Amy and let out a lighthearted sigh.

****

That night as I lay in bed, I thought about how Keisha knew she had to have peace toward all the people who had harmed her, even though it was difficult. I still harbored resentment toward Jon for his betrayal, and my heart still ached for the loss of him in my life. What if he wanted to get back together? What was the right thing to do? In the back of my mind, the question still lingered, "Does one fucked up mistake dismiss all his years of loyalty?" I knew we had become just comfortable with each other the last few years, but didn't that happen to all married couples? I thought of Eric, and realized the intensity I was feeling with him was all part of the honeymoon phase that all new couples go through. But what happens when the fire dies down? Would he eventually get bored and find a new type of excitement? Could a couple survive the daily grind of life? As I was starting to fall sleep, I realized life was a gamble, and it was better to be in the game than not. I was in love with Eric now, and decided it was worth the risk.

Chapter 8

Vicky nervously waited for her parents and sisters to arrive. I had a pot of coffee prepared, and had bought a coffee cake and a box of chocolate chip cookies for them to snack on. I sent the girls to the library so Vicky could have some time alone with her family.

The doorbell rang. I yelled to Vicky upstairs, "Come on down Vicky, and greet your family."

I could hear her pronounced breathing and loud steps as she came down and followed me to the door.

I opened the door to a picture-perfect family. They all looked like they had just returned from church. Vicky's sisters looked around five and seven years old. They were in matching magenta dresses with white sweaters, white stockings and black patent leather shoes, with the front of their long blonde hair held back with butterfly barrettes. Vicky's mom looked like a modern-day Betty Crocker; she was a simple beauty with soft pale skin like Vicky's. Her blonde hair curled against her shoulder bringing out the white pearls that shone against her pink sweater. Vicky's dad looked like a gentle bear. He was burly with broad shoulders, gray hair, and a slightly gray beard.

Vicky's dad greeted me enthusiastically, "Hi there, you must be Shawnsy. Vicky has told us so many good things about you. I'm Bill, and this is my wife Lynn."

"It is so nice to finally meet you," Vicky's mom said, giving me a hug.

"And these are our daughters, Danielle and Becca," Vicky's dad said, patting their heads.

"Hi," they both answered shyly.

"Hello, beautiful," Vicky's father said, while giving Vicky a huge hug.

"Hi, honey, how are you feeling?" Vicky's mom asked softly, while hugging Vicky.

"I'm fine."

"I have some coffee and dessert in the kitchen," I said.

Vicky's dad asked, "Do you mind if the girls watch some TV?"

"Not at all," I responded.

Vicky grabbed the remote. "I'll put some cartoons on for them."

Vicky bent down and grabbed her two sisters in her arms. "I miss you two so much. I'll sit and watch some cartoons with you in a little while."

The four of us sat around the kitchen table. "Can I offer you some coffee or tea?" I asked.

Vicky's dad remarked, "Coffee would be great. We just want to thank you for everything you are doing for Vicky."

"It's my pleasure. Vicky is a very sweet girl," I said smiling at Vicky. She smiled back.

Then Vicky's mother asked her daughter, "I know you have a doctor's appointment coming up soon. Would you like me to come down and take you?"

"It's my ultrasound," Vicky answered.

"That's very exciting. You get to find out the sex of your baby," Vicky's mom commented.

"I think Shawnsy is going to be taking me. Aren't you?" Vicky asked.

"I believe so, but your mother can take you, if you like?"

"Mom, I would hate to see you travel all the way down here," Vicky answered.

"Whatever you want me to do, Vicky. I just want you to know I am here for you," Vicky's mom said.

"I know that, Mom."

Vicky's dad said, "Your mom and I have been talking, and we realized through counseling, that both your mother and I are to blame for how your life has ended up."

"Please don't say that, Dad!"

"It's true Vicky! Your mom got cancer right when you were young and needed her most. Much responsibility was placed on you as a young girl. You took care of your sisters, and helped care for your mother. We vented a lot of our anger on you because your sisters were so much younger than you. We never considered that you were just a kid yourself."

"Honey, we drove you away!" Vicky's mom blurted out.

"Mom, stop it! It's over now. It was their fault, not mine, not Dad's, and certainly not yours."

Vicky's dad said with tears in his eyes, "We want our little girl back."

I started to get teary-eyed, so I purposely stepped away from the table to grab plates and a knife.

Surprisingly, Vicky got up and walked over to her father and put her arms around his shoulders. "I want to come back too! I am so sorry for all the pain I caused all of you. I really am sorry," Vicky said through her tears.

Vicky's mom got up with tears streaming down her face and wrapped her arms around Vicky and her father.

Feeling awkward and out of place, I cut the cake, and gave each of them a piece.

"Thank you so much," her father said, his voice cracking through his tears.

"You're welcome. Do you folks want to be alone? I'm sorry, I should have asked earlier."

Vicky protested, "No, Shawnsy, I want you to stay."

"Vicky, Danielle and Becca are constantly asking about you." Putting her hand on Vicky's hand, her mother continued, "We don't judge you for what you had to do. We feel horrible because of it. We love you so much, Vicky. We just want you to be happy."

"Is that really true, Mom, you don't judge me?"

"Honey, we just want all of us to be a family again," Vicky's mom answered.

"Does that include my baby?"

There was an awkward silence.

"Vicky, your mom and I were talking. We will help you raise your baby, if that's what you want!"

"And what if Mom's cancer comes back?"

There was another awkward silence.

"I really don't know what I want," Vicky remarked.

They all sat there as if there were no more words to be said. "I bet your sisters would like some cookies and juice," I said, looking at Vicky, trying to break the ice.

"Let me go see what they are up to," Vicky said, leaving the room.

All of a sudden we heard squeaky giggles. I got up and stood between the rooms. I watched Vicky tickle her sisters on the floor as they squealed with delight.

It was heartwarming to watch. I knew at that moment, Vicky really was loved and missed by her family.

****

Later that afternoon, Vicky and I were both exhausted. I think the reunion between Vicky and her parents took a lot out of the both of us. When they left, Vicky went to her room and slept.

Keisha and Amy stopped at the house after their time at the library, and immediately wanted to go to the dining hall. I told them Vicky and I would catch up with them because Vicky was still sleeping. I wanted to make sure she was all right after her long afternoon.

Moments later, Vicky waddled down the stairs. She looked like she could have used a few more hours of sleep.

"How are you feeling?" I asked her.

"I'm okay, but I'm still feeling a little tired," she mumbled through a yawn, curling up next to me on the couch.

"The girls are waiting for us at the dining hall. Are you hungry?"

"Not really. Can I skip dinner? I don't feel like eating."

"How about we join them in a little bit? Maybe by then you'll start to feel more of an appetite."

"That's fine," she said, yawning.

"You have a beautiful family, you know that Vicky?"

"I know," she said nodding.

"They care a great deal about you."

"I know that, too," Vicky said nodding again.

"Your parents know how hard everything has been for you. They just want you back and they are willing to help you raise your baby."

"In my heart, I know all that. But as far as my baby goes, I'm not sure what I am going to do."

"I'm sure that everything will work out fine, Vicky," I said squeezing her hand.

"I hope you're right, Shawnsy."

"It will. Now, how about you and I go get something to eat?"

"If you insist."

Chapter 9

I had a whole weekend off, and I couldn't have been happier. I definitely needed a mental break. I spent the whole day getting the house together. I had a romantic dinner planned for Eric and me when he returned from his shift. A chicken parmesan dinner was carefully prepped and ready to go into the oven. My kitchen table was adorned with candles, and my grandmother's good china that I don't even remember ever having used.

I checked my outfit, which I had carefully planned as well. Wanting something sexy, yet classy, I chose a pair of black slacks and a silky purple blouse, with a matching camisole underneath and shiny black stilettos. As I stood in front of the full-length mirror, I actually liked the reflection before me. I hadn't felt this good about myself in a long time. I pulled my hair back in a rhinestone clip and put on a pair of very expensive dangling diamond earrings, courtesy of my sister Gwen. With a few strokes of the makeup magic wands, a stroke of cherry chapstick, and a spritz of Dolce and Gabbana, I was ready for Eric.

I heard a knock on the door. It couldn't have been Eric. I wasn't expecting him for another hour. *"Maybe he got off early,"* I thought.

I opened the door. To my surprise, it was Jon.

"Hi. Do you mind if I come in?"

"Sure," I said, surprised, with an irritated tone.

"You look great," he said, looking me up and down.

"Thanks, Jon." I felt a stirring of anger. In the past ten years, I think he had complimented me twice, and both times he was intoxicated.

Jon looked around, as if he thought the place would have fallen apart since he left.

"Are you expecting someone?"

I ignored his question.

"Jon, what are you doing here?"

"I just wanted to tell you how sorry I was for everything I put you through. I suddenly left and I took away your job. I never planned for any of it to happen. I guess I was just going through some stuff. You know, I'm pushing forty."

I just stared at him. I could feel the tears.

I felt myself getting heated up, and said, "You were my first love. We built a future together, your career, this home. You left me for your twenty-something intern."

"I finally realize Shawnsy, how wrong I was to do that. Stacey and I aren't together anymore, and she left the firm."

"You finally realize how wrong it was?" I could feel my voice rising. "Let me get this straight. You didn't realize it was wrong when you started messing around with her?"

"It all happened so fast. Obviously, I wasn't thinking at all. She was nothing like you."

"I am so very sorry to hear that, Jon," I said sarcastically.

"I have to ask, are you seeing someone?" he asked, looking at the table.

"Yes, I am."

"Honestly, Shawnsy, I didn't think you would start seeing anyone so soon."

"I surprised you, and guess what? I'm thinking about every step I'm taking."

"Shawnsy, you know I still love you. Is there any chance we can be together again?"

"I'm sorry, Jon," I said as I held the door open for him.

Jon walked through the door with his head down. Suddenly, he turned around and we both looked at each other for the very last time.

****

Much to my surprise, I was actually glad Jon had stopped by. Forgiving him had given me a sense of closure. Seeing him one last time gave me a sense of peace about what I knew in my heart all along: that I would never return to him and that I was worthy of someone who would respect me at all times.

****

Eric arrived, and I felt my breath being taken away as soon as he walked through the door. His cologne smelled so manly, and he looked so good in his jeans.

"Hey, sweetheart," he said as he kissed me on the cheek and handed me a bouquet of colorful carnations.

"These are beautiful, thank you so much. Have a seat. I'm going to put these in some water."

"It smells real good in here."

"I really hope you like my chicken parmesan."

"I'm sure it's delicious."

I carefully arranged the flowers on the kitchen table and joined Eric on the couch.

"Listen, Eric, there's something I want to talk to you about."

"What's going on?"

"Jon stopped by earlier."

"Let me guess. He's sorry, he begged for your forgiveness, and he wants you back."

"Well, kind of."

"What is it, Shawnsy?"

"Nothing, I'm not going back to him. But, I am a little confused about some things."

"What kind of things?"

"I don't know; I mean like us, what if this doesn't last? I had so many years invested in my marriage. I'm just a little scared."

Eric took my hand. "Shawnsy, everything in life ends up being an investment, and ultimately a risk. I love you. I love the woman you are. I will do everything in my power to make it work."

"But what if it doesn't?"

"Then life will just keep going on."

"I hope we work, because I love you, too!"

Eric pulled me into his strong arms. His closeness electrified me.

"I am so glad you said that," he said pushing closer into me as we kissed.

****

I lazily woke up the next morning to the sizzling sound of bacon frying and the smell of fresh-brewed coffee, and a 140 lb. Rottweiler lunging at me.

"Go give Shawnsy a big wet smooch, Angie," Eric yelled across the room while busily preparing a surprise breakfast for me.

"What is all this?" I asked, surprised, trying to avoid Angus Beef's wet kisses.

"Breakfast for you, my dear. I tried to be real quiet this morning. I got up hoping that you would at least have some bread and eggs in the house. Shawnsy, you really do have to do a major grocery shopping."

"I know. Getting the ingredients for your chicken parmesan was a major shopping for me. All of this is so nice. I see we have an extra guest."

"I thought it would be too much to ask my buddy to watch her again today. If you don't mind, Angus Beef will be spending the day with us."

"I don't mind at all."

I thought: *I had always wanted a dog but could never own one because of Jon's allergies.*

"Have a seat, my beautiful princess," Eric said, pulling my chair out.

"This is unbelievable. You went to the grocery store, picked up Ms. Beef," I said patting her head as she lay next to me. "Then came back and made this wonderful breakfast."

"It's because you're unbelievable," he said, setting before me a coffee mug and a plate overflowing with toast, eggs and bacon.

"Come here, Eric. This means so much to me," I said, giving him a hug.

"I know it does, and thank you for last night," he said just as he was about to kiss me.

I laughed, covering my mouth. "Stop, I have morning breath."

Eric moved my hand, and kissed me tenderly on the lips.

"Last night was wonderful, Eric, and I also really want to thank you for letting me sleep."

"No problem, but don't be surprised if me and Angus Beef decide to take an afternoon siesta."

"Only if I can join you?" I asked.
"I would love it!"

Chapter 10

Alma explained to me during one of our walks along the campus, 'One of the beautiful facets of St. Agnes' Place is freedom, but it is also one of its most dangerous. The girls are free to leave at anytime. No one is held against their will. All of the girls are taught from the beginning that they are now in control of their circumstances. Many have left throughout the years, never to be heard from again. Most of the girls who stay to the end, flourish. They end up receiving a high-school diploma and are prepared to attend college and mentally able to conquer the real world. Some even become workers in some capacity here at St. Agnes' Place. Graduation is a very beautiful time. It's like watching a larvae turn into a butterfly. The girls' radiate beauty and you can tell how much they want to bring beauty into the lives of others. I know in my heart when they have made it, it's when they tell you how much they want to be a part of the solution to the problems facing so many young women.'

****

"I'm thinking of taking off for a few days," Amy announced to all of us while eating dinner in the dining hall.

"Where are you going?" Vicky asked.

"Come on Vicky. You really need to ask?" Keisha questioned.

"I would like to know where you plan on going, Amy?" I inquired, knowing that she had no family to go home to.

"I just need a break; school is off for two weeks. Anyways, the house will be much quieter without me being here. Keisha can read her books in peace, and I won't be harassing Vicky for always being in the bathroom," Amy said, playing with her spaghetti.

I repeated tersely, "But where are you going?"

Keisha blurted out, "She wants to go see her pimp!"

"Oh no, you really aren't thinking of going back?" Vicky asked.

"I'm going to see a guy I know named Darius," Amy said.

Hoping to convince her, I said, "Amy, please think about it. I know we can't force you to stay here. But, I wish you wouldn't leave."

"Chill out. I'm only going for a few days, and I'm not going to do anything stupid."

"I have a hard time believing that, Amy. You know once he sees you, he's gonna drag you back down," Keisha said.

"I'm not going to let anyone drag me down. Darius practically raised me, and he is all I got besides you guys."

Vicky said, "We are all going to be worried about you."

Amy exclaimed, "Stop, you guys! I will only be gone for a few days!"

"That's what we all thought at the beginning," Keisha said.

****

That night I spoke with Vicky regarding her ultrasound appointment. I knew in my heart that Vicky's parents truly cared for her, and wanted to be a part of her and her baby's life. I felt it was best that Vicky's mom go with her to her appointment instead of me.

"Vicky, your mom really wants to go to your appointment with you. She wants so much to be a part of your life, and your baby's. Would you please consider having her take you?" I asked, sitting beside her bed.

"Oh, my God, Shawnsy feel this," Vicky said, ignoring my question and laying my hand on her stomach.

"I think you have a soccer player on your hands," I said feeling the vibrations of the baby's kick. I was amazed, having never felt a baby kick before.

Vicky said, rubbing her stomach, "I don't know if I will ever see what he or she grows up to be. I'm not even sure yet what I'm going to do."

"You're very lucky your parents are offering to help you raise your baby. That is an option many young women don't have."

"I know, and I've grown so attached to my baby. Whatever decision I make, I know it's going to be hard."

I put the blankets over her and said, "Vicky I will always be here for you, and this little soccer player."

"Or maybe, he or she will be a gymnast, or a beautiful ballerina," Vicky said playfully.

"Whatever it is, I'm sure the baby will be beautiful just like you, Vicky."

"Thank you for everything, Shawnsy, it means a lot."

"So what do you think? Should we give your mom a chance and have her go to your ultrasound with you?"

"I guess so," Vicky said, rolling her eyes and pretending to be unenthusiastic.

I smiled and gave her a kiss on the forehead. "Sweet dreams," I said, happy with her decision.

Vicky bounced back on her bed and said, "Goodnight Shawnsy."

I went downstairs and joined Keisha and Amy, who were sprawled out side by side on the couch watching *Celebrity Rehab*. I decided not to pursue the idea of Amy leaving, hoping she was just having a passing thought.

Keisha said, "I can't believe how stupid these people are, they have so much money and they stick it up their nose."

"If I had their dough, I would be buying me a fancy car," Amy said.

"Amy, you don't even have your license yet," Keisha kidded.

"But I will someday!"

"And that will be the day I move to another state. It's a scary thought—you behind a wheel," Keisha teased her.

Amy just laughed and playfully kicked her.

"Speaking of buying things," I said, interrupting them. "How about I pick up some gifts from all of us and we can have a little surprise shower for Vicky when she returns from her ultrasound appointment?"

Amy commented, "She doesn't even know yet if she's keeping her baby or giving it up."

"Even if she decides to give her baby up, I think the party would make her feel good. Plus, Vicky is going with her mother to the appointment, so her mom can be here for it too, along with her sisters," I said.

"I think that would be nice. I can make her a card and help decorate," Keisha said.

"That would be wonderful, and we can have Alma and Wendy join us. I'll get a really cute cake from Coccadotts and I'll make some finger sandwiches."

"Finger sandwiches, how fancy," Amy said with a fake accent.

"What do you think? Is it a good idea, ladies?"

"I think it's a very good idea, Shawnsy," Amy said.

"You have a good heart, Shawnsy, just like my grandmother," Keisha said.

"Thank you Keisha, that means a lot."

Chapter 11

As I walked the path through St. Agnes' Place, I reflected on my life and couldn't believe that winter was coming to an end so quickly. I still could not believe the turn my life had taken, when six months ago I could barely make it off the couch. The Christmas season had seemed to fly by. My infatuation with Eric was growing into a strong love, not just desire. Although I still had a strong desire for him and I felt myself melting every time he looked over at me and blinked those dark brown eyes.

Eric had asked me to join him on Christmas, and I agreed if only he would share part of the day with my family as well. His family welcomed me as soon as I walked through the door that Christmas day. They were all loud, but with warm, likable personalities. Eric introduced me as Shawnsy, the best thing that has ever happened to him and Eric's dad said I was a dream come true. With that being said, they all raised their glasses and saluted me as Eric presented me with a beautiful opal ring. One of his drunk uncles asked, 'But where's the diamond?' His response was, 'Be patient. This is just the start of things to come.'

I never had given getting married again a thought since Jon and I divorced. I guess I had thought, like Jon, that it would take me a long time to even date, let alone get married again. Eric met my mom and some aunts and uncles as well that Christmas day, and although they weren't as gregarious as his family, they all treated him kindly. My mom shared how wonderful it was to see me so happy. Eric and my mom hit it off immediately, and by the end of the night, he was calling her Mom.

For our final stop that night, we went to visit the girls. It was Wendy's night to work, and we met her and the girls in the gym, where the final festivities were taking place. Eric and I brought gifts for all of them. We had gift cards for Wendy and Alma, books for Keisha, an iTunes gift card and sweatshirt for Amy, and a stuffed bear and charm bracelet for Vicky. To our surprise, Keisha, Amy and Vicky made Eric and me handmade gifts, with cards reflecting on what an impact we have had on their lives. If they only knew what an impact they have had on our lives simply by allowing us the privilege of seeing what was truly in their hearts.

Now, as the northeast snow was starting to melt and the sun was shining longer, I wondered what lay ahead—not only for me and my relationship with Eric, but also for Keisha, Amy and Vicky. I wanted the best in life for each of them. I had developed such a strong motherly bond with the girls, and like a lioness protecting her cubs, I never wanted their vulnerability to be taken advantage of again.

****

I arrived at the house, and there was a feeling of commotion in the air. Wendy was still there, which was strange because usually by the time I arrive, she has taken off in order to beat the city traffic. Wendy was obviously frustrated. She was standing next to Amy who had two huge duffel bags at her feet.

Wendy said flustered, "Maybe you can knock some sense into her."

"Amy, what's going on?" I asked.

"I told you, I'm taking off, for only a few days. It's a break from school. Why can't all of you just leave me alone?"

"Amy, I really don't think leaving here is a very good idea!" I exclaimed.

Keisha interceded, "She's a big girl; she can screw up her own life."

"Not now, Keisha," I said.

"I have to be heading out; I'll let you handle this, Shawnsy. I hope to see you tomorrow, Amy," Wendy said, storming out the door.

"Bye, Wendy," Amy said nonchalantly.

While rocking in her chair, Vicky said, "Amy, I'm afraid if you go, you'll never come back, or something terrible will happen to you."

"Vicky, I'll be back. I just need to see the only person who ever cared about me besides you guys. You're lucky you have your mom, dad and sisters. I have no one but him, and I miss him."

"Oh my God, Amy, I really think you're still in love with him!" Vicky exclaimed.

"Of course she is," Keisha answered.

"Amy, I think you and I need to go for a walk. Girls, you can meet us at the dining hall," I said. I could feel the intensity brewing as I grabbed Amy's arm.

We walked together out of the House of Love. We walked down the path. The sun was strong, as were my feelings. Amy was so stubborn, and young. I just wanted to shake her and tell her what a mistake she was making. I knew Amy loved attention, and the men who gave it to her. But why couldn't she just be happy with the new life she was creating for herself now?

We walked by a large rock with the psalm, "This is the day the Lord has made; Let us rejoice and be glad in it." I thought *how ironic, God gave us this sunny, beautiful day, and I'm sitting here trying to convince a young girl to enjoy her place in life right now, and not walk back into the fires of hell.*

Amy and I took a seat on the iron bench next to the rock. Amy looked straight ahead, avoiding all eye contact with me.

"Amy, we all love you so much," I said turning and facing her as she continued to look straight ahead.

"I know."

"You have come so far. You deserve so much better in life than what this guy has to offer."

"Keisha and Vicky are right; I am still in love with him," Amy said, shaking her head.

"Amy, whatever it is you are feeling, it is not real love," I said gently, taking her hand.

"Maybe it's not, but I really do miss it."

"When you're in love, that guy would do anything for you, not make you do anything for him. If he really cared for you, Amy, he would want the best for you, too!"

"I know, but I just can't shake him. Shawnsy, I never truly felt love from anyone—not from my mom, who walked out on me when I was three years old, the different creeps from my time spent in foster care who just took me in for the money, people I met on the street, nobody. And, the truth is, I don't really don't know how to love anyone, 'cause I never could trust anyone."

"We love you, Amy. We love you so much! And, you can trust all of us. Is there anyway I can get you to stay?"

Amy sat silent.

"Please sit here and think about what I said. I really do love you, Amy, and I want the best for you. I have to go join Vicky and Keisha now," I said through tears and frustration.

I got up and hugged her as hard as I had ever hugged anyone before, and walked away.

****

I met up with the girls in the dining hall. They were eating dinner with Alma and a few other girls from the other houses. It seemed odd, Amy not being there, like a missing piece of a puzzle. Yet I had those same feelings after Leelee was gone.

I was sure Alma and the rest of the girls saw my look of despondency as I made my way to the table.

"Is there something wrong, Miss Stevens?" Alma asked.

"Sort of, I just had a talk with Amy, and I'm afraid she might be taking off."

"There is nothing you or anyone else can do for that matter. We are all responsible for our own actions, right ladies?" Alma asked sternly, addressing the girls at the table.

"That's right, Alma," Keisha said.

"We are all responsible for our own actions, but I pray she doesn't go," Vicky said.

"Praying is the only thing we can do at this point," Alma stated.

"Amen!" Keisha said.

****

After dinner, I suggested that Keisha, Vicky and I go for a walk around the campus. I felt very anxious; Amy hadn't shown for dinner and I knew in my heart that she had made the decision to leave.

The striking orange bushes brightened the landscape of St. Agnes' Place. The sun was warm and bright for mid-evening and as we walked the many paths, the girls did not mention Amy. Maybe they knew in their hearts as well that it was inevitable that she would leave. Along the path was a playground; even in their tweens and teens the girls' derived great enjoyment from it. I believe it made them feel like they were innocent little girls again.

Vicky giggled while whirling around and around in the tire swing. She was starting to really show, and she looked even more beautiful than ever.

"You're going make your baby dizzy," I said, secretly enjoying her doing it. Vicky seemed so free and happy at that moment.

Keisha started laughing as she walked over to push Vicky on the swing and said, "Then the baby will be just like Vicky."

"You're nuts! I'm too heavy now, you can't push me," Vicky said, continuing to enjoy the moment.

"You wanna bet," Keisha said lifting up the swing with all her might.

Both girls were laughing hysterically. For a moment, I forgot about Amy, only to return to the thought that she could be having fun with them as well.

We made our way back to the House of Love. It was empty.

"I guess Amy made her decision," I announced as I walked into the silent, dark house.

"I'm not surprised," Keisha said.

"She should know going back to him is just gonna get her into trouble," Vicky said heading for the rocking chair.

"Amy does know it's wrong, she just doesn't care. On top of that, she doesn't get consequences yet. If she did, she wouldn't be running off trying to be with the man who strung her out. Amy just hasn't hit rock bottom yet," Keisha said, getting comfortable on the couch.

Vicky said sadly, "Rock bottom could be worse than before. She could end up getting herself killed. She could end up dead like Leelee."

"We don't even have a way to contact her, do we?" I asked.

"No, and if we did, Shawnsy, she wouldn't pick up anyway," Keisha said, turning on the television.

I felt restless. I wanted to do something but didn't know what to do. My cell phone suddenly rang. It was Eric. Although I loved every minute I spent with him, I couldn't wait for my time here to end so I could go home, and go straight to bed. He insisted we go out, and that it was counter productive to leave work and go straight to bed on a Friday night. I told him to meet me at my place after work.

I arrived home, and he was already waiting for me at my driveway.

"Hop in," Eric said.

"Eric, I'm really not in the mood for going out."

"Come on, we'll go get a bite to eat."

"I'm not hungry. Amy left and I feel awful."

"Shawnsy, come on, get in the car."

I opened the door and slowly sat down. I felt such sadness in the pit of my stomach.

"Shawnsy, you're new at all of this. This is what happens. I see it all the time. They get rescued, and decide to go back."

"Eric, that doesn't make it less sad."

"You're right, sweetheart. It doesn't make it less sad. I've been in this line of work for so long, I guess I'm kind of immune to it. I can tell who's going to stay straight, or who isn't."

"I can't imagine getting immune to any of this. I feel so close to Keisha, Amy, and Vicky, as if they were my own."

"If over time you don't become immune, you become burnt out."

I understood exactly what Eric was saying, and as much as I didn't want to believe it, he was right.

"Relax Shawnsy, let's just enjoy the night and go for a little ride."

****

I put the windows down a little and the fresh breeze blowing in seemed to calm me, along with Eric's words of wisdom. We headed toward the city. The bright lights on the avenue illuminated the shops, and it was enjoyable just looking into the small privately-owned shops with the bay windows in front. Most of the shops were urban retail and stayed open late hours.

"I am going to have you experience tonight two things I know you have never experienced before," he said.

"Huh, so you think you know me that well?" I asked, feeling my mood starting to lift.

"I think I have a pretty good handle on you, Shawnsy."

I looked over at him. His personality turned me on. He wasn't cocky or conceited, just amazingly confident.

We parked on a side road off the main avenue, and walked the city street.

"You are going to have the best cheesecake you ever had—Cheesecake Machismo," Eric said.

"Geez, you seem to know the best of everything."

Eric suddenly grabbed me from behind, and put his broad, tight arms around my shoulders and rocked me back and forth, giving me a deep, wet kiss on the neck.

"Shawnsy, I do know the best of everything, I got you, baby," he said, letting go of his embrace, but now playfully digging his fingers into my waist.

It was so nice what he was saying; I actually felt ticklish, and all I could do was giggle.

"Now, let's go have our cheesecake," Eric said.

We entered a small eclectic shop that had 70's and 80's memorabilia hung on the walls. Two incredibly kind, tattooed workers greeted us at the front door.

Eric and I each ordered a slice of funky-flavored cheesecake, and a cup of coffee.

As I sat at the bistro table, taking my first bite of cheesecake, I thought, *Eric really does know the best of everything.*

After we had devoured our cheesecake, and drank our coffee, Eric said it was time for our next adventure.

"Where are we going? It's getting late."

"Oh, you'll see."

I couldn't imagine where we were going.

We started to leave the city and headed toward the suburbs again. Eric slowly turned down a winding path.

"I bet you have no idea where I'm taking you."

"I have no idea, Eric."

"How about this? I will give you three clues."

"I'm ready. What are they?"

"It's a place with three hots and a cot."

Before I could answer him, a big red glowing sign appeared: Colonie Heights Women's Correctional Facility Ahead.

"What, are you kidding me Eric?" I asked, clearly confused.

"I want you to meet some lovely ladies. And I might want to show you off to some of the COs I know."

"What is this about? I thought you were taking me to two really great places. And, after the first place was so great, I kind of thought the second place would be great, too."

"Shawnsy, you weren't listening. I said I had two things for you to experience tonight."

"I never in a million years would have guessed this place."

"You just might enjoy yourself."

I followed him up to the secured gate. I couldn't question him anymore. I figured I would just follow his lead.

Two rather obese men in security greeted Eric as if they were long lost friends.

"Is there any chance we could have a few minutes with Tayla Rivers and Misty Jones? My friend Shawnsy here just started working with troubled youth at St. Agnes' Place, and I think she could benefit from talking with them."

"Sure, I could take care of that for you, Detective McDermott," the less reserved of the two officers said.

The officers handed us security badges and pressed a loud buzzer that welcomed us through the front corridor.

The smell of urine and feces was overwhelming and I had to keep myself from putting my sweater over my nose. I felt scared, even though it was obvious how secure the facility was. I had to keep reminding myself I was with Eric.

We ventured into a visitor's area which was furnished with old worn-out tables and chairs.

"Aren't we going to talk with them through glass?" I asked concerned, hoping the space between us would serve as a barrier of protection.

"No, Officer Calhoun will bring them down. He'll be with us, they'll be cuffed, and they are nothing to be feared."

In the background, between the pulsing buzzers and the clanging of metal doors, we heard the echoes of cries and the distant sounds of anger.

Officer Calhoun arrived with Tayla and Misty.

"Hello ladies, thanks for taking a few minutes to speak with us. Shawnsy, this is Tayla and Misty," Eric said kindly.

"Shawnsy just started working at St. Agnes' Place and I thought I would have her meet the two of you alumni."

"Detective McDermott, I wish we didn't have to meet here," Tayla said.

Tayla's voice was strong and deep. Her eyes radiated sadness. Her head was bald except for some slight nappy hair that was starting to grow in and her skin and teeth looked like they had been neglected for years.

"You and your team tried saving me, St. Agnes' Place tried saving me. I just kept making the same stupid mistakes. I kept saying next time I'm gonna do things differently, but I kept going back to the streets, and I'd be doing the same old shit," she said.

"In the end, who's the only one that could ultimately save Tayla?" Eric asked.

"I guess that'd be Tayla. I knew the right path, I didn't before I came into contact with you or my time spent at St. Agnes' Place. You all set something inside me; I just needed to follow it. I guess the key word is I. I didn't listen, and I made some really bad choices. And I got myself five years for it."

"What makes you think when you get out in five years that things will be different?" Eric asked.

"Because I'm forty-two years old, I can't afford to waste another day."

"What about you, young lady?" Eric asked, looking straight at Misty.

Misty was a younger version of Tayla, except her hair was done in braids and she had slight acne and crooked teeth.

"I know, Detective McDermott, I kept doing wrong. But I'm gonna be listening to you all when I get out of here. I'm gonna get my cosmetology license while I'm here. I'm gonna get me a job. I'm gonna do the right things from now on."

I smiled at her. She shyly smiled back.

Eric sat back in his chair. "Ladies, I would like to thank you for meeting with us, and I hope I don't see you ladies ever again, except maybe at a beauty salon." Eric smiled and looked at Misty.

"You come to my salon someday, and I'll do your hair for free," Misty said.

"I'll remember that," Eric said with a grin.

"Detective McDermott, thank you for everything you did for me. I'm sorry I have to thank you from here," Tayla said.

Eric patted her on the shoulder. "You thank me again when you get out of this place by staying clean, and keeping out of trouble."

"I'll do that. I promise. By the way, is Ms. Alma still around?" Tayla asked.

"Ms. Alma is still there," Eric said.

"Will ya give her a big hug for me?" Tayla asked, her deep voice becoming sad. "I really love that woman."

"I definitely will. Take care of yourselves."

"Thank you, ladies," I said.

As the ladies were led away, I turned to Eric. "Yes, I get it! I can only do so much. Can we get out of here now?"

"I'm glad you're getting it, Shawnsy, because you would never make it in the long run at St. Agnes' Place if you didn't. Plus, I like you working there; I get to stop by and keep my eyes on you," he said childlike, putting two of his fingers to his eyes then to mine. "Before we leave, I just want to stop and see a CO that I know."

"Fine, but can you make it quick, I really don't like hanging out here. It's not really where I want to spend my Friday night."

"Did you forget about the cheesecake, the world's best, might I add. And, my love, the night's not a complete bust yet," Eric said, putting his arms around me.

"Eric, I'm so tired. I'm about to steal a cot."

"If you want a cot I'm sure one of these lovely ladies would share one with you."

Eric said suddenly, "Hey, look who's here. I was just going to look for you."

"Detective McDermott, long time no see. How ya doin?"

"Good. I want to introduce you to my girlfriend, Shawnsy. She works over at St. Agnes' Place. Shawnsy, this is Officer Mike Miller. I got to know him well when I worked in Homicide. I brought Shawnsy here to meet some ladies that have been provided help in the past, and show her that sometimes there is only so much one can do."

"It's nice to meet you Shawnsy, and listen to Eric. He has been around a long time and he has seen just about everything," he said, extending his hand to me. "How's life on the street, Eric? You have a tough job on your hands. I bet it's worse than working Homicide?"

"It has its challenges. By chance, did Edita Ardiss get paroled yet?"

I thought: *Ardiss. That is Keisha's last name!*

"Man, she got paroled, and ended up back here again. I tell you, Eric, some of these women really like it here," Officer Miller said.

"Mike, I think it's you they come back here to see."

"I'm starting to think you're right."

"Is there any way we can go speak to her real quick? She's the mother of one of Shawnsy's girls."

"I don't see why not, it's almost time for lights out, so I'll just walk you to her cell. I believe she has the place all to herself."

I whispered to Eric, "Is that Keisha's mother? Why are we going to see her?"

"I thought you might want to tell her how wonderful her smart-ass daughter is."

While walking to her cell, I clung close to Eric's side, as seductive remarks were screamed to me from every direction. Like animals trying to claw out of a cage, arms from every direction reached out to touch me. I tightly grabbed onto the back of Eric's shirt as we made our way to the cell.

"Settle down, ladies," Officer Miller yelled at the top of his lungs as he led us to her cell.

"That's one pretty girl, Officer Miller," an inmate remarked as we passed.

"See Shawnsy, they think you're pretty," Eric said, trying to be funny.

I ignored him.

"She's mine, ladies," Eric announced.

The cell block became a choir of "Awws."

"Eric, I'm going to kill you," I whispered, trying not to look up, while continuing to hold onto the back of his shirt.

"You would do no such thing, Shaws, because then you would really end up here."

"Eric, you're really something else."

We arrived at Edita Ardiss' cell. The buzzer clanged, and the metal doors opened abruptly, startling Edita as much as me. Edita was sitting at the edge of the bed in a manly fashion, reading what looked to be a Bible. She was muscular, and much older than I would have expected. She looked to be in her late fifties, with mocha colored skin like Keisha's. Unlike Keisha's long shiny hair, what little hair her mother had was covered by a white du-rag. Pictures of what appeared to be a young Keisha were taped along the wall.

"You have company," Officer Miller shouted.

"Hello, Edita, I don't know if you remember me, it's been a few years. I'm Detective McDermott," Eric said, introducing himself.

"I'm sorry, I don't. But I was probably pretty wasted," she answered politely in a deep voice. "What can I do you for Detective?"

"Are those pictures of your daughter, Keisha?" Eric asked, looking at each picture.

"Yes, they are. Is my baby in trouble?"

"You're daughter is doing wonderful. This is Shawnsy, she happens to work with your daughter at St. Agnes' Place."

"You know my Keisha?" she asked solemnly.

"Yes, your daughter is an amazing and strong young woman. She's doing very well. In fact, she is one of the smartest girls on campus."

"That little shit has always been smart," she said, looking down, lost in thought.

"Edita, we happened to be in the neighborhood and we thought we would let you know your daughter is doing really well and you should be very proud of her," Eric said.

"I miss my baby girl so much; I haven't seen her in so long. I got my Bible here, and I know Jesus loves me and forgives me. I hope Keisha will someday do the same."

"Now it's your turn to make her proud," Eric answered.

"I'm gonna try, Detective."

Eric signaled to Officer Miller to open the cell.

As we were leaving, Edita looked up and said, "Would you tell my baby girl I love her and I'm gonna do her right when I get out of here?"

"Will do," Eric answered as we walked out of the cell.

"Hey, Detective, I guess I didn't do too bad, Keisha's a good girl."

Eric just turned around and gave her a look.

****

We left the jail. I understood deep inside what Eric was talking about. All of these women knew the way, and the old adage, "You can lead a horse to water but you can't make him drink it," was so true. I will impart direction from now on, pray for their guidance, and hope that they choose the right path, and accept that in the end it's all in their hands.

Chapter 12

There was a good energy in the air at the House of
Love; it was the day of Vicky's ultrasound and baby shower.
Vicky's mother arrived with her two younger daughters. It
was so nice to see them again. Vicky's mother had a southern
charm about her, minus the southern drawl, and Vicky's
sisters were poised and lady-like. I offered to have Vicky's
sisters' stay at the house during the appointment. I figured it
would give Vicky some time alone with her mother to discuss
the baby, and her sisters would have a good time helping
Keisha and me decorate.

As soon as they left, Eric arrived with my mother, her
box of homemade food, and a huge gift bag filled with baby
toys.

Eric handed me the bag and said, "I couldn't resist. I
love baby toys."

I had invited my mother; she had heard so much
about the girls and she loved to cook so I thought it would be
a nice way for her to meet all of them. Keisha made her way
through the bags of baby decorations I had carefully hidden.
Eric and I had barely a moment to speak before Keisha
started directing him to get the step stool and hang pink and
blue crepe paper, while she and Vicky's sisters hung paper
teddy bears. My mom made the dining room table into a
buffet, with a pink tablecloth and blue overlay, and carefully
arranged her food and my finger sandwiches, while I set up
the cake table and punch bowl. Wendy arrived and brought
chocolate teddy bear favors, and placed them next to the
teddy bear cake that I brought. Alma arrived with a fruit salad
and a couple of Vicky's friends from the other houses.

Everyone brought gifts, and what touched me most was the card that Keisha wrote; written in bubble letters, was how much we all love Vicky, and how blessed we all were to know such a kind-hearted, sweet and sensitive girl. She wished her the best with the baby, and that it took a "Real Mommy" to know what was really best for her baby.

The moment arrived and Vicky and her mom walked through the door. We all yelled, "Surprise!" Vicky was gushing with delight and genuinely surprised. I had her take a seat in the rocking chair, and pinned a pink and blue carnation on her chest.

"Come on, we're dying to know!" Keisha yelled out.

"You're not going to believe this, but my mom and I decided to let it be a surprise," Vicky said, beaming.

"I can't believe you didn't find out," Keisha said, disappointed.

"I'm sorry, but we do know everything is progressing as it should be," Vicky's mother said.

My mom made the announcement that lunch was ready and that the beautiful lady with baby should lead the way. We all fixed our plates, while Vicky's mom took pictures of everyone.

Before the gifts were opened, Vicky thanked her mother for going with her to her appointment, and thanked all of us for showing her such love and acceptance.

"My mom and I had a real heart to heart talk today, and we both realize that at this point we aren't sure what's going to happen to this little person," Vicky said rubbing her stomach, and fighting back strong emotion. "But I know my baby will surely be loved, and have a lot of really cool things. I want to thank all of you from the bottom of my heart for everything."

With each gift opened, there were oohs and aahs. I was surprised Eric stayed, although hidden in the corner. He looked comfortable and not out of place among the women. When Vicky opened his bag of toys, he carefully explained with delight what each toy did.

After the gifts, Vicky posed for pictures around the cake. Suddenly, the front door opened. It was Amy. The room suddenly became silent. Amy looked shocked upon seeing everyone.

"Wow, look who's here," Keisha said.

"You're just in time for cake, Amy," Alma said, directing her to an empty chair.

"Amy, you're back," Vicky said.

"This is your time, Vicky. We have all night to talk to Amy," Alma said.

I went over to Amy, and without any words being spoken we hugged each other tightly.

After Vicky kissed and hugged everyone goodbye, I thanked her mother for taking Vicky to her appointment.

"Shawnsy, I thank you for everything. I think I have my daughter back," she said, smiling, with her arms around Vicky.

"I love you, Mom, and I'll see you soon," Vicky said, hugging her.

"You two girls be good," Vicky said, bending down and hugging her little sisters.

"We're always good!" they both answered in unison.

"I know that," Vicky said, patting their heads.

I casually said goodbye to Eric. I told him I would text him later about Amy's time away.

As soon as all the guests cleared the house, except for Alma, and Wendy, all eyes were on Amy.

"Girl, you're back. I can only imagine where you've been," Keisha said.

"Oh, there's no place like home," Amy answered, lost in thought and visibly shaken.

"Do tell," Keisha said.

"That day when I was packing my bag I was thinking about how much I missed Darius, and the excitement of the streets and hanging out at the clubs. I always thought I was his girl, his favorite. When I stepped off the bus downtown, I felt euphoric. Then I walked down the main street, the sounds of dogs barking, loud music and fast cars were like music to my ears! I made myself look real good for Darius; I had me a tight tank top under my hoodie and some tight-ass jeans. I had my hair all down, and Darius has never seen me with my natural strawberry hair. I thought he'd be liking it. I strutted up the steps to the run-down brownstone I used to stay at with him. I rang the bell, knowing that it was mid-afternoon and he would probably just be getting out of bed. When Darius opened the door, you'd think he'd seen a ghost. 'What are you doing here?' Darius asks me.

"I told him I was just stopping by to see him. Darius starts looking me up and down and asks, 'You still at that home?'

"I said I was. The smell of stale beer and pot became stronger as I followed him into his second-floor apartment. I was shocked to see how cluttered and dirty his apartment was. Dirty laundry was scattered all over the place, and empty beer bottles lined the countertop. Sitting out on the coffee table in plain sight was one of his many Smith and Wessons. His place hadn't changed a bit since I last saw it; it was really strange for me to see because I haven't been around that type of environment in so long. 'You ready to come back?' Darius asks me.

"That question made me feel real good! I was like, damn, he really does miss me!

"I ask Darius, 'You mean live here?'

"Darius has the nerve to say to me while opening a beer without offering me any, 'Yeah, you can live here. But you gotta make us some money.'

"I got real pissy ass with him and said, 'You mean make you some money!'

"I never talked back to Darius before. I felt real nervous after saying that to him.

"He very sarcastically says to me, 'Bitch, if it wasn't for me you would have been dead.'

"I told him, 'Darius, I was dead when I was with you.'

"Darius asks me, 'Then what brings your sorry ass back here?'

"At this point I was trembling and I say to him, 'I was actually excited about seeing you.'

"Truth was, even though I was nervous as hell, he was still turning me on.

"I finally was able to get the words out and said, 'Now as I sit here, I feel bad for you.'

"Darius started laughing and asks me 'Ho, you feel bad for me?'

"I started to really break down. I could barely speak, but I told him, 'I'm no ho.'

"Darius looked at me and said, 'You're a ho, you always gonna be a ho.'

"I swear at that moment I saw the devil in his eyes. I don't know what came over me! Without thinking I got off the couch and grabbed his gun off the coffee table. I was trembling, so I could hardly hold it. That motherfucker just sat there like nothing was happening, and asks me, 'Now what the fuck are you going to do with that?'

"I looked at him square in the eyes, and said, 'I thought I was special to you, but I really was just one of your whores. Sick as it was, I loved you. I loved you even though you made me feel worthless about myself. I even loved you when I walked through that door. Now I want to blow your fucking brains out.'

"Darius started screaming, 'Bitch, you ain't gonna do nothing but put that gun down, and get your ass in that bedroom!'

"When I heard that, I lost it! I cocked the gun. For the first time, I saw panic on Darius's face. I pulled the trigger. The bullet hit the couch. I was so scared, I dropped the gun.

"Darius jumped off the couch and lunged at me, screaming, 'Stupid bitch, I'm gonna kill you.'

"I turned and ran as fast as I could out the door. I was in such a panic, I fell running halfway down the stairs, and all I could hear was Darius screaming from the top of the stairway and at the top of his lungs. 'You stupid bitch ho, you'll be back, you'll be back.' I kept running and running until I could hardly breathe, but for the first time in my life I felt free."

Keisha cheered, "You're getting it girl! You're really getting it!"

Amy let out a nervous giggle, which was a welcomed relief to the terrible flashback she had just shared with us.

"Too bad you didn't kill the bastard," Keisha remarked.

"Keisha, we're glad she didn't, or we would be visiting her behind bars," Alma said.

"Oh Amy, I'm glad you're back," Vicky said, giving Amy a hug.

"I'm sorry you had to go through all of that. Maybe you needed to go back there to realize you don't belong with Darius and his world," Wendy said.

"Thanks, Wendy, I think I get it now."

I was shocked that Amy was sitting there among us.

"Amy, you put a real scare in me," I said.

"I'm sorry, Shawnsy. I'm really sorry," Amy said almost inaudibly.

Chapter 13

I was so glad to have the next few days off. Eric decided that it would be a nice idea to get away and visit the Jersey Shore. It sounded wonderful. I hadn't been to the Jersey Shore since I was a little girl with my parents and sister Gwen. I still remember Gwen and I burying each other in the sand, and the fun we had strolling down the boardwalk and sharing curly fries.

We arrived at Wildwood, New Jersey, and we were welcomed by the shrill sound of the seagulls and the warm, fresh ocean air. It was an unusually hot day for the end of May. Eric turned the air on as soon as we walked into the room. We were both very tired; the drive down took longer than anticipated due to a backup on the Jersey Turnpike. Eric and I jumped into bed. The cool air felt wonderful, and the reflection of the sun shining through the curtains gave the room a peaceful ambience. Eric and I fell asleep in each other's arms. It was a refreshing nap that gave us the energy needed to conquer the rest of the day.

"Thank you for bringing me here. This is so nice."

"The weekend has only just begun," he said, pulling my body into his.

Our lips locked and our bodies started moving like thunder. I wanted to swim in his cologne, and eat his body. His mouth devoured every part of my body, and the intensity I felt was overwhelming. Upon completion, his head was buried in my hair, and with his final stroke were the words, "I love you, Shawnsy, I love you so much!"

"Me too!" I answered, breathlessly.

****

That evening the sun cooled down, and the boardwalk was alive with people. The continuous warning to "Watch the tram car, please," repeated itself like a broken record to the mass of people deeply enthralled by the sights and sounds of the shops and sidewalk performers. We walked hand in hand slowly along the boardwalk, the breeze billowing off the ocean engulfing us. When I wasn't taking in every moment of being the woman lucky enough to have Eric by my side, I looked to the beautiful majestic blue waters of the Atlantic Ocean below the deck. Each pier was lined with novelty and t-shirt shops, similar in nature. Eric and I went into each one with the enthusiasm as if we were searching for a pot of gold. We each bought t-shirts sporting the Wildwood logo, and trinkets for the girls, and Eric bought every New York Yankees t-shirt that he could find. We were together as not only lovers, but best friends. We were both giddy and in love.

"We definitely have to go in here," Eric said.

"Eric, this is a tattoo parlor," I said, questioning him.

"Maybe I'm thinking of getting another tattoo."

"Is this place even legal?"

I truly loved the two tattoos Eric had; I always found myself running my fingers down them while we were together, as if the ink would rub off. The tattoo on his forearm was of a bald eagle, which he had done after one of his friends had died during a tour in Iraq. The other one on his shin was of a cross, which he explained was for faith.

"You want a tattoo, Shawnsy?" Eric asked, teasing me.

"I don't think so, Eric."

Page 91

"Oh, come on, you can get "Eric" written across your tramp zone in big letters."

"My what?"

Eric rubbed his hands along my back; it sent chills down my spine.

"Right here, Shawnsy. Did you think I was calling you a tramp? Oh, you can just be my tramp."

"Yep, that's exactly what I want to do, so I can be branded like an ox. Oh, and if we ever split up, I get to have your name there forever."

In an instant, Eric's mood changed. "Let's just get out of here," he said.

I followed him out of the parlor to a ledge overlooking the ocean.

"What's wrong?" I asked, even though I knew why he was so upset. I should never have mentioned if we should ever break up.

Eric looked truly hurt and asked, "Don't you believe in us?"

"Eric, I am so sorry, it just came to my mind—people I have known throughout the years that have former lovers printed on their bodies."

"Shawnsy, I didn't know we were like those people."

I felt so bad inside. I never meant to hurt his feelings, the very man I couldn't believe I was walking arm in arm with.

I put my hands on his face. "Eric, we're not. Truth is I don't want a tattoo. Is there anything else I can do to put a smile on your face?"

"Yeah, you can go on that big Ferris wheel with me," Eric said with a sly smile, pointing to the Ferris wheel overlooking the pier.

"That's not fair, Eric!"

Eric grabbed my arm. "You said you would do anything to put a smile on my face."

"Wait, that's not what I had in mind! Do you want to see sweet little ol' me in agony? You know I hate heights. I couldn't even have us stay in a hotel room past the fourth floor."

"I actually could bear to see you in a little bit of agony right now."

"Oh, you're real nice, Eric."

Eric put his arms around me and said, "I need to hear from you, Shawnsy, that this is the real thing between us. I need to know we're together for the long haul."

"Eric, I love you more than anyone. I can't imagine life without you, and yes, yes, yes, I am ready to spend the rest of my life with you."

"I needed to hear that. I'm not going to get down now on one knee and propose, because first I have to finish saving for a ring. But, I am glad to hear that I will get a big yes when the day comes."

I kissed his soft lips. "Do I still need to go on the Ferris wheel?" I asked, hoping he would have changed his mind.

"Of course. Now, let's go!"

"Now this might not be that good of an idea, what if I have a panic attack and die, you'll be without your wonderful bride-to-be."

"I'll take that chance."

We stood before the Ferris wheel. An old burly man who looked like a farmer slowed the seat before us. "Lucky number seven," he said, lifting up the bar. "Enjoy the view."

I thought: *Enjoy the view! I would just be happy not to pass out.*

"Eric, I'm so scared."

"Oh, Shawnsy, look out. You can see the pretty ocean," he said, swaying the seat.

"Eric, stop that!"

Eric put his hand over mine. "I'm sorry. I didn't mean for it to do that," he said, grinning.

"I can't believe you made me go on this!"

"Shawnsy, don't ever question us again."

The seat stopped at the top. I sat rigid. Eric pulled me closer to him. Normally, that would have taken my breath away, but being stopped 150 feet up along with the jarring of the seat made me feel a heightened sense of anxiety.

"Eric, I never questioned us. I love you so much," I said quietly, hardly able to speak because of my nervousness at being stopped at the top of the Ferris wheel.

"Now, that's what I love hearing," Eric said as the cart descended.

Finally, the ride came to an end.

"Do you want to ride it again?" Eric asked.

I just shook my head, waiting for my anxiety to calm down.

Eric teased the old farmer, "She just loved it. We'll be back again later."

Eric pointed in the direction of the rollercoaster, "That was fun, and you survived. How about we go on that rollercoaster?"

"How about not! I think you owe me an ice cream," I said, trying to regain my equilibrium.

"I guess I can do that," he said, returning to his sweet self.

****

We arrived at Stewey's Ice Cream Stand. We each ordered a vanilla ice cream dipped in chocolate on a sugar cone. We sat on a bench together, eating our ice cream, watching the motley crew of people pass us by. From the corner of my eye, I saw a little girl scream as her cartoon balloon blew to the sky. It reminded me of what I was trying so hard to possibly explain away to myself the past few months; that I could possibly be pregnant.

****

When we returned to our hotel room, it was freezing. We had left the air-conditioning on, not realizing that the humidity would ever die down. We both put on comfy sweats in anticipation of the fireworks that go off every weekend at sundown starting in May.

After changing, I went to the bathroom. I reached down and grabbed the concealed pregnancy stick wrapped like a mummy in toilet paper out of the trashcan. I sat at the edge of the toilet and stared at the two blue lines. Thoughts raced through my mind: *Could this really be possible? Should I tell Eric now, or when we return home? I know Eric loves me, and I love him, but a baby before marriage, and so soon after my divorce? And worst of all, having to tell my mom, Gwen, and everyone at St. Agnes' Place.*

"You fall in there, princess?" Eric asked from outside the door.

"I'll be right out," I yelled back. I quickly wrapped up the stick, threw it back in the trash can, and flushed the toilet.

I stood before the mirror, took down my ponytail and brushed my hair while trying to reclaim my composure.

I came out acting as if nothing was wrong. Eric went into the fridge and popped open two ice-cold beers for us to enjoy out on the balcony while we gazed at the fireworks.

"Here you go," Eric said, handing me the opened bottle.

"Oh, no, thanks. I'm really not in the mood," I answered, hoping he wouldn't inquire any further.

"Just take it and sip at it," Eric said persistently, handing me the bottle. "Maybe I want to get you good and drunk and take advantage of you."

"I don't think you have to get me drunk," I said putting down the beer and wrapping my arms around him.

"Let me put this down for a minute."

Eric pushed me onto the bed. All my anxious thoughts were pushed aside. Being with him was intoxicating, his hands and mouth moved in a sequenced rhythm. I rubbed my hands along his sweaty body. His body was beautifully tanned except for the parts that only I was privy to. The background noise of shooting stars and thunderous bangs played like synchronized music to the ups and downs of our bodies in motion. One loud bang was heard, and Eric exulted in a final thrust that left us both breathless. Our bodies lay knit together as we were both too exhausted to move.

"You think we can catch the finale?" Eric asked.

"Maybe, if we move quickly," I said, wanting so badly to catch the best part of the fireworks, but not wanting to end the pleasure I had in Eric's arms.

"Okay, one-two-three," Eric said, holding my waist and lifting me off of him.

We both put our clothes on, like young children being late for school.

Eric grabbed his beer and I grabbed mine without thinking.

We made ourselves comfortable on the patio chairs, as the cold ocean air blew through our hair. The fireworks ripped through the sky in designs of red, orange, and blue. Deepening the sky were long lines of rainbow colors and shooting stars sprinkling down that left Eric and me in awe.

With the last bang that left us craving for so much more, I turned to Eric and slowly said, "Eric, I'm pregnant."

"Are you saying what I thought you said?"

"Yes. Oh my God, are you upset?"

"I'm not upset. I'm-I'm-just shocked. I can't believe it."

"I haven't had my period in two months, and I took a pregnancy test here, and it's positive."

"Two months, and you took a pregnancy test here?"

"I was in shock myself. I was told I couldn't have children years ago when I was diagnosed with endometriosis."

"I can't believe this, Shawnsy; we're going to have a baby! Are you happy?" he asked while giving me a hug.

"I am, but I have to admit I am a little worried what people might think, especially my mom and Gwen, and everyone at St. Agnes' Place. Not to mention, I haven't been divorced that long."

"Your mom and your sister both love me, so who cares?"

"And what about the girls and Alma at work?" I asked.

Eric put his arms around me and said, "Shawnsy, it will all work out, I promise."

"You're right, and honestly, Eric, it's a baby made with you. What more could I ask for?"

"I love you Shawnsy, and I love this little peanut," Eric said, rubbing his hands over my stomach.

In his excitement, Eric whisked the beers off the side table and handed me mine. He proudly raised his beer and made a toast. "To us and our little guy!"

"Eric, I don't think I should be drinking. And who says it's going to be a little guy?" I asked playfully, sharing in his enthusiasm.

Chapter 14

Eric and I returned to his apartment in upstate New York. Although we had shared a beautiful time away, the thought of how our lives would be changed forever overpowered the memories of the crystal blue waters of the Jersey Shore. We both agreed it was best that my pregnancy be kept a secret for now.

When we arrived, we were greeted enthusiastically by Angus Beef who leaped off the couch straight to Eric.

"Hey, big girl! Did Danny-Boy take good care of you while we were gone? We missed you, and guess what? You are going to have a little baby brother or sister," Eric said in a baby voice while petting the hyper dog. Angus Beef barked and yipped as if she were actually responding to the big news.

"Shawnsy, do you mind if Angie knows?" Eric asked while the dog jumped up and down.

"I think she can keep a secret."

"I don't know about that. Angus Beef is a woman."

I laughed and collapsed on the couch. I wasn't sure if it had been the long car ride that made me feel exhausted, or my pregnancy. Eric recommended that I spend the night at his place. I agreed I was too tired to move, nonetheless unpack, and I had plenty of clean clothes left over. The plan seemed wonderful, and as I closed my eyes I started to feel myself fall into a peaceful sleep accompanied by the sounds and smells of the heavy panting from Angus Beef, who had decided to share the couch with me.

****

The next morning, I decided to return to my quiet home, drop off my luggage, and pay some bills. I finished all my tedious chores earlier than expected, and although I was anxious to see the girls, I felt a sense of uneasiness continue to weigh upon me about revealing the news to my mother. I hadn't had this sense of fear since Jon was my first love during my college days and we feared the worst during our many "accidents." Now fifteen years later, it felt like "déjà-vu all over again."

I arrived at my mom's home. The strong aroma of garlic and the sound of olive oil spattering in the pan engulfed me as my mother opened the front door.

"Why, what a pleasant surprise! You are just in time for some spaghetti and meatballs," my mother said enthusiastically, while giving me a huge hug.

"I don't have much time, but it sure smells good," I said, wanting to swim in the deep aroma of the simmering spaghetti sauce.

I had actually been craving spaghetti sauce the past few weeks, and while away, I had more pizza and sausage and pepper sandwiches than I had ever had in my lifetime.

"Let me get you some," my mother said, while grabbing a large bowl.

We sat at her tiny kitchen table and I wanted to dig in, but I also knew I couldn't keep my pregnancy news in for another second. "Mom, I'm pregnant!" I blurted out.

"You're pregnant. I thought…?"

"Obviously I can," I interrupted her. "I'm sorry if I disappointed you."

"I'm going to finally be a grandmother!" my mother shouted, and raised her arms up.

My bowl of spaghetti and meatballs almost tipped over from her sudden vibration.

"I take it you're not upset?" I asked.

My mom gently put her hand upon mine. "Shawnsy, are you all right with all of this?"

"Yes, I am. I really am, and I really do love Eric. We plan on getting married, but I don't know when."

"Then that's all that counts. Do you remember how you felt almost a year ago? See, you never know what the good Lord has in store for you in this lifetime. And, I would bet Eric is beaming with joy."

"He is. He really is," I said, feeling her joy and a great sense of relief.

"Mom, can you let Gwen know the news?" I asked lowering my voice as if others were actually listening.

"I'll let her know, and she will be fine with it, but maybe just a little jealous," my mother said, with a big grin.

I smiled back. "Thank you, Mom."

"For what? Now eat your spaghetti and meatballs. You're going to be late for work," my mom said, shoving the bowl closer to me.

****

It was a bright shining Saturday afternoon in May and my mom's reaction to my news made the day even better. I arrived at the House of Love hoisting a menagerie of hair clips, shell necklaces, and t-shirts that I picked up for the girls at the boardwalk. The girls greeted me with open arms, and acted like it was Christmas as they sprawled together on the floor to go through the assortment of goodies.

"How was your weekend away?" Keisha asked while laying out all the hair clips in an orderly fashion.

"It was very nice," I said, watching with delight as they sifted through the large bag.

"Thank you, Shawnsy, for thinking of us," Vicky said.

"Oh yeah, thank you, Shawnsy," Amy said as if she had forgotten, being so consumed with the contents of the bag.

"You're the best, Shawnsy," Keisha said.

"Why, thank you; and seeing it's a sunny Saturday afternoon and we have no plans," I started to explain.

"I know you want to take us to the movies!" Amy interrupted with excitement.

"No, that's not exactly what I had planned."

"Oh," Amy remarked, disappointed.

"Your moving-up ceremony is coming up, and I thought you girls would like something nice to wear for it," I said, as the girls continued to be engrossed in the bag.

"Did you know for all our clothes, and even nice clothes for court or special events, we just go through the bins at Charity House?" Keisha asked.

"I know, but I am so proud of you girls, and it seems like forever since I have gone shopping. I was thinking of having you ladies pick out some pretty dresses, on me."

Amy, Vicky and Keisha turned away from the bag, and looked at me with disbelief.

"Are you serious?" Amy asked.

"Yes, I'm serious!"

Keisha said, "Man, girl, you really are the best!"

"Shawnsy, that's very nice of you, but my mom buys all my clothes and we already have my dress picked out for the ceremony," Vicky said, very appreciative of my offer.

"Would you mind coming along for the ride?" I asked.

"It sure sounds fun!" Vicky said.

"All right Cinderellas'! Get your slippers on. It's time to go find dresses," I announced.

We arrived at Ursula's of Switzerland, the place I thought I would never see again since leaving Jon. Every year Jon and I went to the prestigious NYS Attorneys Ball and Jon made sure that my dress came from there, and he made sure everyone else knew where I purchased it as well. I never truly minded. It was the one time that he never cared how much I spent, the dress was truly for show, and they did have the nicest dresses in town.

The girls jumped up the steps and looked into the bay window. A row of mannequins poised in rainbow sequined dresses gazed upon us. The dresses were exquisitely beautiful.

"I want that dress," Amy shouted.

"I want that other dress," Keisha said.

"Oh, my gosh, I want to get a dress so bad," Vicky said with a little disappointment in her voice.

"Girls, there are a lot more dresses inside. Let's go check them out," I said, sharing in their enthusiasm.

"Good afternoon, ladies. How can I assist you?" Ursula asked in a strong Swiss accent.

Ursula was in her late seventies. I remembered her from my youth, greeting my mother and me as we looked for my prom dress.

"My girls and I are looking for some dresses for their moving-up ceremony."

"Congratulations, ladies. We have several racks over there that are specifically for young women," Ursula said, pointing to the corner.

"As for you young lady?" Ursula asked, looking baffled at Vicky.

"I'm not getting one today," Vicky answered.

"I see," Ursula said, nodding in agreement. "Once you beautiful ladies find what you like, I will measure you. Let me know if you need help in anyway."

Keisha and Amy jetted over to the racks while Vicky and I sat in the chairs reserved for those usually paying. Keisha and Amy pulled down dress upon dress.

"I think I found one," Amy announced. It was a silky emerald green dress that made her strawberry colored hair look radiant.

"That dress is so beautiful," Vicky said, encouraging Amy.

"I like this one," Keisha said, holding a sleek, satiny apricot dress that contrasted perfectly with her deep mocha skin.

Ursula yelled over to them, "Ladies, those dresses are exquisite, now go try them on and see how they look on you."

"Why don't you go help them out?" I asked Vicky.

"I will, but I sure wish I didn't have my dress already."

I smiled at her. This was my opportunity to take a quick peek at the wedding dresses.

"Can I help you with anything?" Ursula asked.

"Oh, no thank you. Just looking," I answered, not wanting to draw any attention to myself.

"Shawnsy, come in here and check this out," Keisha yelled from the dressing room.

I walked over, wishing I had more time to check out the racks of wedding dresses.

"You look so gorgeous in this," I said, putting my hand on her waist and feeling the smooth satin. I checked out the price, and it was exactly what I had planned on spending on each of them.

I watched Amy in the center of the dressing room admiring herself in the mirror. The dress was contoured to her slim body perfectly. She looked so proud, turning side to side, staring quietly at her reflection. I didn't want to interrupt her. I wanted her to seize the moment, feeling beautiful and classy.

Ursula entered the dressing room with measuring tape in hand. "I see beautiful princesses!" She rubbed her hands down the seams of both dresses. "I believe you have found the perfect dresses. No work for me." Ursula smiled and folded up the measuring tape.

"Did everyone get what they wanted today?" Ursula asked, looking at Keisha and Amy.

"We sure did!" Amy said.

"Thank you so much, Shawnsy," Keisha said.

"Thank you, Shawnsy. I love this dress!" Amy said while twirling in front of the mirror.

Although it had been a perfect day so far, as I walked out of Ursula's I couldn't help thinking while staring back at the rack of bright white wedding dresses, I really had not gotten what I wanted.

****

I met Eric at his place, and I told him about my mom, and about treating Amy and Keisha to new dresses for their moving-up ceremony.

"You are so good to those girls. They are so lucky to have you."

"I am so lucky to have them. They got me to stop focusing on my own problems. And, speaking of problems, it's a big load off of my mind that my mom is all right with everything."

"Shawnsy, I knew your mom loved me. See, it wasn't as bad as you thought. You forget you're not eighteen anymore."

"I know, but we're an old-fashioned family."

"And, we're in love," he said, pulling me closer to him on the couch and wrapping his arms around me.

"I know, but even today looking at wedding dresses made me sad."

"I thought you were looking at dresses for the girls?"

"I was, but they also sell wedding dresses."

"Oh, do you want a white wedding?" Eric asked playfully, while twirling my hair.

"I don't think I could get away with that."

"I don't think you will actually be showing by then."

"You're such a dork." I laughed. "Unless we are planning the wedding for next weekend. Of course I will be showing. And, I don't even see a ring on my finger," I said, raising my left-hand.

"I see what this is about," Eric said, getting more comfortable on the couch and putting his head on my stomach.

"What are you doing?"

"I thought I heard the baby, but I think you're just hungry, Shawnsy," he said, kidding around.

I started to feel myself getting heated up, and I wasn't quite sure if it was my hormones or Eric's refusal to take me seriously. I impatiently pushed his head off of me.

Eric suddenly sat up and looked at me trying hard to contain his anger. "I had something romantic planned for us, but I guess you just can't wait," Eric said, jumping off the couch and heading toward his bedroom.

"Eric, wait!" I yelled, "I really do want something romantic, I'm so sorry."

Eric stood in the doorway, and slowly asked, "Would you like me to give you the ring right now?"

"No, Eric, but can you at least give me a date and some direction of where we are going?"

"Shawnsy, I want you to be my wife as soon as possible. I don't care where we get married; I will leave the details of all of that to you."

"Eric, there are some things I want to be clear about. Are we going to live here or at my place? What are we going to do once the baby is born? I can't continue to work the shift I'm working. Can we afford for me to stay home?"

"It would only make sense to stay at your place seeing that it's paid off," he said wisely. "That kind of answers whether we can afford for you to stay home, but do I really want us to raise a family in the home of your prick ex-husband? And this place is just an oversized bachelor pad. I think the best thing for us to do is to live at your place, and eventually buy a new house with a nice big backyard."

"With a white picket fence?" I asked.

"Whatever you want, Shawnsy," Eric answered, clearly exhausted.

I put my arms around him, and hugged him hard. I didn't want to let go. "Thank you, Eric," I whispered in his ear.

Chapter 15

Something about the charming surroundings and the landscaped paths leading up to the House of Love engulfed me with an aura of lightness and positivity. But today I felt differently as I walked the paths, a bittersweet feeling seemed to consume me. I couldn't help thinking of the conversation Eric and I had, and the fact that I would be staying home full-time to raise our child. I'd grown so attached to Keisha, Vicky, and Amy and I still thought about Leelee everyday. I pictured her smiling and dancing with the angels, but most of all I thought of her as being free—free from the demons that she could not shake. I also felt a sense of loss, knowing that Keisha would be attending an elite boarding school, Vicky would be rejoining her parents and raising a child, and Amy would be the only one left. She would eventually be joined by more girls and hopefully her walls would be broken down, and she would become more vulnerable as time went on. I believed Amy allowed Keisha, Vicky and me to get as close to her as much as she could emotionally surrender. They all would be taking the next step in their lives, steps that were needed in order to mature, and ripen their lives to any possibilities that awaited them. Maybe I needed to focus on that as well.

I opened the door to the sounds of silence, yet all three of them were sprawled in various positions in the living room. Amy was sitting against the couch with her iPod, banging her head in rhythm to the music. Vicky was rocking in her rocking chair with a washcloth on her face, and Keisha was engrossed in her notebook.

"Why is it so quiet in here?" I asked.

"Keisha is working on her speech for the moving-up ceremony," Vicky said quietly.

"Keisha, you've been asked to be a speaker? You must be so thrilled. That is such an honor!"

"I am honored; I have the highest overall average. But now I have to get up and talk in front of everyone," Keisha said, making an exaggerated pouty face.

"I would never guess that you would have a problem with that!" I teased her.

"You're developing a sense of humor, Shawnsy," Keisha said.

"It's about time, isn't it, Keisha?" I asked, my mood feeling lighter.

Keisha laughed and shook her head as she made her way to her bedroom.

"Hey, Miss Vicky, what's ailing you?"

"I have such a huge headache. I never, ever got headaches until I was pregnant."

"I know what you mean."

"Huh?" Vicky asked.

"Oh, honey, is there anything I could get you for your headache?" I asked, praying that she would just ignore my last comment.

"No, but if you can, please just pull this baby out of me. I can hardly move anymore."

"I know, honey, your baby will be coming soon enough."

I still couldn't believe that Vicky, whom I regarded as just a child herself, was carrying a baby just like me. I wanted to ask her so many questions, but I knew I would just blow my cover.

"I am going to have to waddle up to the stage to get my diploma. It's going to be so embarrassing," Vicky said, trying to get more comfortable in the rocking chair.

"No, it won't. You should be so proud of yourself. You successfully made it through the school year."

"Whoopee! And the great news is next year I get to go to a regular school while raising a child."

"Your parents are going to be there for you and your baby every step of the way. You will have school dances to look forward to, and different events. Everything is going to work out fine."

"You really think so, Shawnsy? How many guys do you think are going to want to go out with a sixteen year old with a baby? Not to mention my Lifetime-Movie-of- the-Week past! Plus, I want a nice guy like my own daddy."

"You are so beautiful, Vicky—inside and out. You are probably the sweetest girl I have ever met. Trust me; it will all work out for you."

I was sincere in what I said to Vicky. I truly believed that in the end, it would work out for her. I just knew the road to getting there was going to be a long one for her, and it saddened me to think that she would have to endure anymore pain in her life than she already had. But, it would take a special guy to look beyond her past, and love her for the beautiful person she truly was.

"Hey, Shawnsy," Amy said, taking off her iPod.

"Hi, Amy," I said, as she ran to the kitchen.

I turned to Vicky, who still looked like she was in pain. "You decided you are going to keep your baby?"

"I guess the decision has already been made for me. I told my mom while we went shopping for my dress for the moving-up ceremony that I liked Winnie the Pooh. Actually,

I told her I like Classic Pooh, and the last time we spoke, she said she had a nursery awaiting us in Classic Pooh."

"That was very nice of her."

"It was very nice of her, but it sure put an end to the discussion of whether or not I'm keeping my baby."

"The decision is ultimately up to you."

Vicky sat up and started rubbing her stomach, "You're right. It is because my baby's daddy is long gone, and who knows where he is. Thanks to my parents, I certainly don't need his money. But I must admit I really have grown so attached to my baby. I know my parents will raise it along with me, and my baby will lack for nothing. I just feel so scared right now, Shawnsy."

"I understand, but you have plenty of people who love you and will be there for you. Trust me, it will all work out."

"That's what faith is all about," Keisha announced, coming down the stairs with an open book.

"Shawnsy has great faith in you. She can feel it. I have faith in you too, girl!" Keisha said.

"Thanks, Keisha. I'll try to have a little faith," Vicky said.

"I didn't have any faith until I came here. I just knew survival. St. Agnes' Place taught me faith is all you really need."

"You're an inspiration to us all, Keisha," Amy yelled from the kitchen.

"Thanks, Amy," Keisha said, rolling her eyes.

"Keisha, I have to talk to you about something," I said feeling anxious. "Detective McDermott took me to a jail one night. It's a long story, but your mom was there and I met her."

"You went to a jail and you saw my mother? Why did you go see my mother?"

"We didn't go there specifically to see your mother but, Detective McDermott somehow knew that she was there."

"He knows, Shawnsy, because she is always there!"

"Your mother wanted me to tell you that she loves you very much, and that she is really going to try harder when she gets out. Keisha, I'm sorry. I should have told you sooner. Things have just been so crazy."

Keisha yelled, "That bitch is crazy!"

"I understand how you must feel. I just wanted you to know your mom seemed very sincere," I said, feeling a little frightened by Keisha.

All of a sudden, Keisha angrily slammed her book shut. The loud thud startled all of us.

"Detective McDermott really knows how to show you a good time, Shawnsy!" Keisha said while storming back up to her bedroom.

"I'm so sorry, Keisha."

Vicky looked over at me with a sympathetic smile. I felt horrible.

"Maybe she should have a little faith," Amy yelled from the kitchen.

Vicky yelled back, "Amy, that's not very nice. And why are you making macaroni and cheese again? You're going to make me sick!"

I felt terrible inside for upsetting Keisha, but I felt I had to tell her about her mother. And the smell of macaroni and cheese was starting to make me nauseous as well.

****

After refusing to join us at the dining hall for dinner, Keisha finally emerged from her room. Her eyes were bloodshot. Despite her tough, confident exterior, a young girl full of feelings existed.

"Would you like me to get you something to eat, Keisha?" I asked softly.

"I'm not hungry."

"When you do get hungry, I will be more than happy to get you something," I said, smiling gently at her.

"Can we just go for a walk?" Keisha asked.

"Sure, ladies, would you like to go for a walk with us?"

"I would love to go, but unless you guys have a wheel barrow to take me along, I really don't think I can make it," Vicky said, losing her breath.

"Vicky, I really don't think we would be able to push it," Amy said.

"Thanks, Amy. Shawnsy, please make sure you take her with you."

"Vicky's orders, Amy. Now go get your shoes on."

Amy started to walk toward the kitchen.

Vicky yelled, "Amy I know you're thinking of putting some popcorn in the microwave to take with you! Weren't you? You know the smell makes me sick!"

Keisha said, her mood lightening, "Damn, girl! You would think you're the pregnant one. You can sure put it down."

"What can I say, I love to eat, but it ain't doing me no damage," Amy said, rubbing her hands down her body.

"I don't know about that. You got some big-ass booty going on back there," Keisha said.

"You got some ghetto booty yourself!" Amy said playfully, smacking Keisha's behind.

****

It was a beautiful crisp spring night, and the scent of lilacs perfumed the air.

The girls brought a basketball with them, and bounced it back and forth to each other while we slowly made our way through the campus.

We stopped at the play area. We had the playground and basketball court all to ourselves.

The girls played their own version of "horse" while I made myself comfortable on a park bench.

I loved the banter between the two of them. They giggled and acted silly while emulating each other's moves. Although they mostly chided each other, I truly believed they had each other's back.

"Come on, Shawnsy, get out here and show us what you got!" Keisha yelled over to me.

"I don't have much."

Keisha threw me the ball; I dribbled and attempted to make some shots.

"You have just a little bit more than Keisha," Amy said.

"You think so? How many games of horse did I beat you in?" Keisha asked.

"Those games don't count. We didn't spell the whole word each time; we just spelled "ho,"" Amy said, and both of them started laughing.

"Shawnsy, can you do me a favor?" Keisha asked, throwing me the ball.

"Anything. What would you like?" I asked, trying my best to make a basket.

"Will you never, ever, bring up my mom again?"

"I won't, and I'm truly sorry. I didn't mean to upset you."

"I know you didn't. Can I ask you a question?"

"Of course."

"Do you really think that people can change?"

"Sure, I believe people can change."

"Do you think my mom can change?"

"I thought you didn't want her mentioning your mother?" Amy asked sarcastically.

I shook my head at Amy.

"Ladies, I can't talk and play basketball at the same time. You two are wearing me out. Let's go sit down."

Amy asked, "How about we go sit on the swings?"

We walked over to the playground area and put our feet in the warm sand while we made ourselves comfortable on the swings. The spring air was whisking through their hair while they rocked backed and forth. They both looked so beautiful, their faces glowing with childlike innocence.

"Yes, I truly believe your mom can change, Keisha, if she tries hard enough," I told her while swinging back and forth.

"I really thought I had forgiven my mother. But I guess I still feel so angry at her. She always says she's going to do better and then keeps messing up. How many times should I forgive her?" Keisha asked.

Amy answered, "Seventy times seven. That's what Alma says."

"I think that's what the Bible says, too," I said.

"It just seems like everyone in my family is messed up. It's like a curse that keeps going down the line from generation to generation. I hope none of my kids ends up messed up," Keisha said.

Amy laughed and asked, "You pregnant, too, Keisha?"

"You know what I mean; it all just has to end."

"Keisha, by being aware of the cycle and trying so hard to live a good life, you're putting an end to the curse."

"I hope you're right, Shawnsy, but I don't think I have it in me anymore to forgive."

"I know it's very hard to forgive people sometimes, but you do it for yourself. That doesn't mean you are excusing them from their wrongdoing," I said.

"Did you forgive your ex-husband?" Keisha asked.

My stomach sank as she asked the question.

"Yes, Keisha, I think I can finally say I have forgiven him," I answered, although those words were hard to say. "It took me awhile, but I forgive him. I finally realize however way he wronged me doesn't make up every part of him as a person. I just choose not to have him be a part of my life anymore."

"That's sort of how I feel about my mother."

"A marriage is much different. You're a part of your mother. Not having her in your life is a really big decision. Sometimes people just need some boundaries in their relationships, especially when the relationship has been damaged," I explained.

"What do you mean?" Keisha asked.

"Maybe you can have a relationship with your mom someday; it doesn't have to be close at first. You can build on it, take baby steps with it. Lay down some conditions, or rules, and if both of you follow them, who knows what will happen."

"That's not a bad idea. Thanks, Shawnsy," Keisha said, pondering what I said while continuing to swing back and forth.

Amy said, "Shawnsy, you're lucky you have a really nice mother."

"You're right, Amy. I am lucky," I answered, realizing how often I forgot how lucky I was to have her, especially during this time of my life.

Amy turned and looked intently at Keisha. "Keisha, even though your mother's a fuckup, you're lucky. At least she wants to change and be a part of your life. I don't even know where my mother is, and I doubt she would even recognize me if she saw me."

Keisha got off her swing and put her arms around Amy. I got up and joined them.

Chapter 16

"Shawnsy, we are only going away for a weekend. Did you pack your whole wardrobe?" Eric asked, struggling to lift my bag.

"Oh, come on, you're a big alpha male. You can handle it," I said, opening the door for him.

Eric suggested we take a relaxing weekend trip to Vermont, which was just an hour from our home in upstate New York. I had the whole weekend off, and Eric said he had time he had to "use or lose" from work, but I was hoping the meaning of this trip was for an even greater purpose.

Picturesque mountains, old churches, antique shops and silos greeted us at every turn. We arrived at the Merry Top Inn; it was a quintessential old Bennington mansion. We were greeted warmly by a middle-aged couple who kindly introduced themselves as Richard and Pam. Pam asked if there was anything specific we were interested in doing while we were here.

"We just want to kick back and have a relaxing time," Eric answered.

"We can certainly promise you that. If you should get tired of relaxing, we have some wonderful museums, art galleries, and of course, our beautiful rivers and streams," Pam said.

"It all sounds so nice," I said.

"I know there has to be a bathing suit somewhere in that big bag," Eric said, pointing to my bags which Richard, the innkeeper, had picked up.

"Actually, there are two big bags, and two bathing suits. Whether they fit or not is another story," I said with a chuckle.

"Be careful carrying them, buddy. I don't want you to break your back," Eric said.

I gave him a flirty hit on the arm. I was feeling good, and was excited to see what the weekend would bring.

We arrived at our room. It was painted in sage green and had an old-world, royal feel to it.

"This is so beautiful," I said, admiring the beautiful antique furnishings.

"It is beautiful, and it is also haunted," Eric said, animatedly twinkling his fingers in front of me.

"Get out," I said, although I wasn't quite sure if he was serious or not.

"I heard there was a ghost that roams the corridors here at night," Eric whispered.

"Now who told you that, Eric?" I asked trying to figure out the authenticity of his claim.

"I heard it before from my old sergeant, Dicky Brower."

"Oh great. I hope for our sake they are friendly ghosts."

"Yeah, maybe Dickster is one of them. He just passed away last year," Eric said while unpacking the bags.

"You're crazy, and what would be even crazier is a ghost named Dicky," I said while lying back on the bed.

Suddenly my bathing suit hit me in the face.

Eric said, "Good catch!"

"What do you want me to do with this?"

"Put it on."

"Where are we going?" I asked, not wanting to leave the cozy bed.

"Fly fishing."

"What?" I asked, getting up suddenly.

"I knew that would get your butt off that bed. I thought you might want to try some inner-tubing. I thought it would be nice and relaxing."

"That actually does sound nice. And you're sure there is no degree of danger? You do remember our baby is in here?" I asked, rubbing my stomach.

"No danger, unless I decide to tip you over," Eric said, putting his arms around my shoulders and swaying me.

"Eric, I really don't think you will be able to lift me now, and I really hope this bathing suit still fits," I said, turning around and pushing the suit into his chest.

****

We arrived at White River. My black bathing suit clung to every curve of my body. I definitely looked pregnant or extremely bloated at best. The heat was intense and the blue water looked so inviting. Eric helped position me onto my tube and jumped onto his with great ease. We relaxed in our tubes with our arms afloat, embracing the simmering sun as it beat on us. We were both silent, enjoying the peacefulness of the river. The only sounds we heard were crickets dancing in the tall grass and a group of Boy Scouts in the distance.

Eric grabbed my toe, and brought me closer to him. He kicked some water on me, but I didn't mind at all. It was cool and refreshing, and I did the same to him. Our tubes twirled in motion to the lazy river.

All of a sudden, I felt the baby kick as if he were bored by the gentle motion of the waves.

"Eric, this is heaven," I said, calming the baby with my hands.

"Shawnsy, anytime I am with you, I feel like I'm in heaven."

****

We arrived back at the inn. I took off my wet bathing suit, which was clinging uncomfortably to my body, and I stared at my nude body in the dresser mirror. My breasts were full and my stomach was protruding, *but at least I got a great tan,* I thought. Eric made a beeline for the bathroom. The toilet flushed, and I heard the pipes crackle, and a sudden burst of water.

"Shawnsy, why don't you and McGillicuddy come join me?" Eric yelled from the bathroom.

"I'll ask him. McGillicuddy said yes—so here we come, but we have to use the potty first." The annoying urge to pee was now hitting me every hour, on the hour.

"Just don't flush the toilet," Eric yelled from behind the curtain.

"I won't," I said, quickly finishing my business.

The shower was lukewarm and ran down our sweaty bodies as we pulled closer to each other. We gently kissed, and Eric slowly worked his way down my body. He grabbed my stomach in both his hands as if he was grasping a basketball and gently kissed our child.

****

After getting dressed, we both decided we were starving.

"How about we go get a bite to eat?" Eric asked.

"That sounds wonderful."

"There's a nice country eatery that I heard is real good, not too far from here," Eric said.

"Are there ghosts there, too?

"No, I haven't heard anything. I think it's ghost-free."

"In that case, let's go. I could sure go for a nice juicy burger," I said, hearing my stomach growl.

****

We could smell the charcoal burning as we pulled into Big Bob's County Kitchen. We walked into a country store with shelves of homemade barbecue sauces and maple products that led to the eatery. Long tables adorned with brightly colored tablecloths and fake flowers awaited us. There was an enthusiastic mood there, which was made even greater by our vivacious waitress. She let us know that Big Bob really existed and was the best rib maker that ever lived, as surely as she was born on a cattle farm in Texas and Flo was her real name. It still didn't convince Eric and me to order the ribs. Although we truly believed her, we decided to go with burgers and fries.

We devoured our burgers and fries as if it was our last supper. Eric and I both agreed that we may never know if Big Bob's has the best ribs, but they certainly had the tastiest burgers we have ever eaten.

"When do you plan on telling Alma and the girls you're el- prego, and it's my baby?" Eric asked, while slurping the remains of his milkshake.

"I really would like to wait until after graduation, and after Vicky has her baby; but I'm afraid if I wait any longer, they are all going to start thinking I put on a few," I said, picking at the last of my fries.

Page 122

"You can start borrowing some of my shirts. That should conceal our secret," Eric whispered.

"Great idea, Eric. Do you think it's going to be a big secret you're the father?" I whispered back.

"I don't know. Maybe they will think you and Jon had one last rendezvous."

"That's not funny," I said, throwing a french fry at him.

"What do you think Sir Jon is going to think when he finds out you're pregnant?"

"I actually think he is going to be sad. I believe reality or karma is going to touch him in ways he probably hasn't felt in a long time. It's a fatal blow to the heart when the person you want back in your life is carrying someone else's child," I said, feeling surprised at the ache in my heart I had for him.

"Karma is a real bitch, isn't she?" Eric asked, accenting the "she."

"Whoever said Karma is a she? I asked. "Seriously though, I really do feel bad for him."

"What?" Eric asked, with a confused look on his face.

"I am finally at a place of divine happiness. I guess when you reach this point in life; you want the best for everyone else as well. I can sit here right now and say I sincerely hope he finds true happiness."

****

We arrived back at the inn as darkness had set in. I took Eric's advice and changed into one of his long t-shirts. It was loose and comfortable, and had the scent of Eric on it. My clothes were starting to feel tighter, and I finally came to the realization that I needed to start shopping in the maternity section. I brushed my hair and realized it had become a much dirtier blonde as my pregnancy progressed. As I looked into the mirror, I noticed a pretty girl staring back at me. My face was clear and glowing, and I actually appeared more youthful than a year ago.

I opened the French doors that led to a balcony overlooking the majestic grounds. The onyx sky was clear, and the bright white full moon stood out among the cluster of stars.

"Do you think it's a good idea to be smoking out here?" I asked, seeing Eric sitting with his head down, taking drags off his cigarette.

"I'm sitting on the third floor balcony; there's no one staying below us."

"How do you know?"

"I'm a detective, remember?" he looked over at me with his beautiful brown eyes.

"That's right, how could I have forgotten," I said, lying back in the lounge chair next to him.

"Plus, I was feeling a little nervous," Eric said, putting his cigarette out in a plastic bathroom cup.

"What on earth are you nervous about?" I asked, staring up at the moonlight sky.

Eric got up. "Give me your hand."

I felt a rush of intense excitement, thinking: *is this what I think it is?*

Eric took my hand and led me to the wall of the balcony.

"I love you so much, and I love this unexpected little guy so much, too!" he said, putting his hands on my stomach.

"I love you so much, too!"

Eric got down on one knee and pulled a box out of his pocket. "Shawnsy Stevens, will you do me the honor of marrying me?" he asked, taking a sparkling diamond ring out of the box and gently putting it on my ring finger.

"Yes, I would be honored to be your wife!"

Eric got up and kissed me. My heart was racing a mile a minute; I grabbed the top of the cobblestone wall to hold myself up. I looked deeply into his eyes which radiated love and kindness. "I love you so much Eric, more than you could ever know, and I can't wait to be Mrs. McDermott," I said with tears in my eyes. Eric grabbed my limp body and lifted me off the ground into his strong loving arms.

Chapter 17

"Shawnsy is getting married, Shawnsy is getting married," my friend Kristen stammered drunkenly.

"Again," Michaelann said tipsily, while raising her wine glass.

It had been close to a year since I had seen my two dearest friends whom I met in college. Kristen's newest business venture was selling jewelry of African safari animals. Before that, it was European spices and Korean cutting knives. Although she only dabbled in all of her ventures, it always ensured that we would get together at least once a year. I missed the camaraderie the three of us once shared, but work, children and failed marriages seemed to have kept all of our lives extremely full, and unfortunately that left little time for our friendship.

Kristen had her share of ups and downs during the past few years, which included the death of her mother and her own divorce. She apologized for not being there for me as much as she would have liked, but at the time, her own feelings were still raw. Dealing with her two teenage daughters on top of everything else was overwhelming. I understood, and secretly harbored feelings of guilt as well for not being there as much for her, but work and distance seemed to rule my life at the time. I looked at Kristen. She was trying so hard to get her groove back, and it was working. Her once-chubby figure was now incredibly thin, which she claimed was the one good thing that came about from her divorce and subsequent depression. She now looked like a sexy mama, rather than a soccer mom. Her face was made up, her jet black hair was now accented with light brown highlights, and although she was inebriated, Kristen seemed to be feeling comfortable in her own skin.

As the last of the suburban housewives started to leave, we sat in the corner catching up on each other's lives.

Kristen asked, "Let me get this straight. You now work with hookers, and you're soon-to-be husband is the man who saves them?"

"I wouldn't call them hookers," I answered, while Kristen and Michelann finished a bottle of white wine.

"So—what would you call them?" Kristen inquired.

"Sluts!" Michaelann blurted out.

Michaelann was a tough but generous and kind-hearted Sicilian with glowing olive skin and short spiked coffee-colored hair. She was fun-loving, with a dry sense of humor that was unleashed whenever she had had a few too many, which I clearly remember from our college days. Life had been good to her; she had married her college boyfriend as well. Unlike Jon and I, they were still going strong. Michaelann ruled the roost, but Marty seemed to go along merrily, always trusting in Michaelann's good judgment. They had two sons and a daughter, and when they weren't busy running them around, they were involved in some sort of home improvement project on their old country home.

"That's not nice. Most of the girls where I work are under sixteen and at that age they can't even legally consent to having sex. They are all victims, usually coerced by a pimp," I said.

Michaelann laughed and said, "And Eric is the pimpanator."

"I guess you could call him that." I laughed along with her, never having thought of Eric that way.

"Well, I wish you both a long and happy life, like me and my Martin," she said, raising her empty glass and saluting me.

"Do we get the privilege of being bridesmaids for the second time?" Kristen asked.

"I would be honored to have you both as bridesmaids for the second time. But seeing it's both our second time around, I think we are thinking something more low-key, like a ceremony with a justice of the peace and an outdoor barbeque," I answered, not really sure if Eric would even consider this idea, but he had said whatever I wanted.

"When would you like all of this to take place?" Michaelann asked.

"I definitely would like to have it in the next few months."

A sudden feeling of anxiousness came over me; to pull off a small affair in the next few months would take immediate action.

Michaelann said, "What? A few months? We haven't even met your fiancé."

"I know, but he just proposed to me last week, and," I paused. "I'm pregnant!"

"You're pregnant!" Michaelann and Kristen said, almost in perfect harmony.

Kristen asked, "What? I thought you couldn't…?"

"Surprise—obviously I can."

The two sat drunk, speechless, and in an utter state of shock.

"I knew there was something fishy going on. You didn't want to partake in our wine, and you look like you put on a few," Michaelann said, while checking out my body.

"I know. I'm starting to look a cow and I'm just getting through my first trimester."

Kristen asked, with a look of hurt in her eyes, "Shawnsy, why didn't you call us?"

"Honestly, things have been moving so fast. I really did want to call and tell you sooner. But now that I am here with the both of you, I have to tell you I'm starting to feel real nervous."

"Is it about the baby?" Kristen asked.

"No, it's actually about the wedding. I have so many details I have to take care of and I sure could use some help from the two of you, if you don't mind?"

Kristen smiled, looking over at Michaelann. "Absolutely. And Shawnsy, we really are happy for you. Aren't we, Michaelann?"

"Of course. Whatever you may need, Shawnsy, we are at your service. You can even have it here, if you like?" Michaelann asked, playing with her wine glass.

"And my brother can do the catering. He still does it on the side," Kristen said.

"We would be more than happy to help you out with the invitations and anything else," Michaelann stammered.

"You two are wonderful. Thank you so much. Kristen, consider your brother hired, and I will let you know, Michaelann, if I take you up on your offer," I said, as my cell phone vibrated. I picked it up. It was Wendy. Vicky's water had broken and she was on her way to the hospital.

"I hate to break up our little party, but I have to go," I said getting up and giving them each a big hug.

"Is everything all right?" Kristen asked.

"I hope so. One of the girls in my care is on her way to the hospital."

"What happened?" Kristen asked.

"Her water broke."

"She's going to have a baby?" Michaelann asked. "Geez, you ladies really do have interesting lives. Now I definitely need more wine."

We all burst out laughing.

****

I quickly arrived at St.Vincent's, a large hospital not far from St. Agnes' Place. A stout, older woman, whose voice and wrinkled skin seemed to reveal that she had smoked way too many cigarettes in her day, led me to the birthing center, which was on the other side of the hospital in its own private wing. The wing resembled more of an ivy-league college campus center than a typical city hospital. Knotty-pine wood floors glistened, and a large colorful mural of a child embraced in his mother's arms stood out behind the nurses' triage area. Leather sofas and chairs were situated in private rooms off different corners of the floor. Soft jazz music whispered in the background, while the smell of baby powder scented the air.

I turned the corner and heard familiar giggles. Amy was pounding her fists on a vending machine.

"Keep pounding away, Amy. They all might come flying down," Keisha said, looking up from the magazine.

"Stop that Amy, and sit down," Wendy said.

"Hi girls," I greeted them. "How is Vicky?"

"She is only three centimeters, so it's going to be awhile. Alma is in with her right now," Wendy answered.

"Has her mom and dad been called?" I asked Wendy.

"They're on their way; it will take them awhile to get here."

"Hey, Shawnsy." Amy came over and gave me a bogus hug. "We are starving. You think you can hook us up with some chips?"

"Of course, Amy, because you're so gosh darn sweet."

I reached in my purse, and surprisingly found six one-dollar bills. I handed the money to Keisha, who was absorbed in a magazine.

Amy said, "Thanks, Shawnsy. I ask and you give the money to her."

I laughed at her silliness.

"Shawnsy, we could use some pop, too," Amy said.

"Of course, Amy, that should be enough money. I certainly wouldn't want to see you two go thirsty."

"Wendy didn't seem to care," Amy said.

"That's not true, Amy. I didn't expect to be coming here today, and I usually don't bring money to work."

"Don't you trust us, Wendy?"

"Of course I do."

"Please eat these," Keisha said, bending over and grabbing the bag of chips from the dispenser and throwing them at Amy. "It might shut you up."

"I want to go check on Vicky. Did you girls see her yet?" I asked.

"We saw her; she was in a whole lot of pain. Alma wouldn't let us stay with her," Keisha grumbled, eating a chip out of Amy's bag.

"Get your own damn bag," Amy said, turning away from Keisha.

"You should see the puddle she left back at the house, its nasty," Amy said, with her mouth full.

"We will have Wendy clean it when we get back," Amy whispered and smiled, pointing to Wendy, who was staring straight ahead in her own little world, unaware of what Amy was saying.

I smiled back at Amy, thinking to myself *what a good idea*.

"Wendy, do you mind showing me to Vicky's room?" I asked.

"Not at all."

"Can I trust the two of you to sit here and behave yourselves while I bring Shawnsy to Vicky's room?"

"I promise we will try our best not to kill each other," Keisha answered.

"And, if we do, the good news is we are at a hospital," Amy said.

****

Wendy led me to the room. Vicky was lying back in bed. Alma sat close to her bedside.

"Hi, sweetie, how are you feeling?" I asked.

"It hurts so bad, Shawnsy."

"I know it does," I said, giving her a hug.

"Hi Alma."

"Hello, Miss Stevens, the nurse who just left said that if she walked or took a shower she might feel better and it might help her dilate quicker," Alma said, rubbing Vicky's leg. "Shawnsy is here now, Vicky. You can walk with her if you like. Why don't you give it a try?"

"I just want some drugs and they won't give them to me yet," Vicky cried.

"I know, honey. Soon enough you will get them," I said.

"Shawnsy, I have some phone calls to make. Would you mind taking care of Vicky for a while?" Alma asked.

"No problem. I am here for her," I said, stroking her sweaty hair back.

"Vicky, why don't you get up and go for a walk with me? Keisha, Amy, and Wendy are sitting in the lobby. They are anxious to see you."

"I'll try."

I helped her out of bed, and we walked arm in arm out to the lobby.

"Now, doesn't this feel better than just lying there?"

"You're right," Vicky said, barely able to talk.

We turned the corner. Amy was bouncing up and down, doing the Charlie Brown dance while listening to her iPod. Wendy sat stone-faced, as Keisha combed through a tabloid magazine.

"Look who's here," I announced.

"Hey, girl," Keisha said, getting up and giving her a gentle hug.

"Vicky, aren't you excited?" Amy asked her.

"No," Vicky said barely audible.

"It will be over before you know it," Wendy said.

"I wish I could take this pain away from you," I said, rubbing her back. "Why don't we walk a little more, and then we'll go back and get you in a nice hot shower."

Vicky didn't answer me, she just continued walking. Seeing her in such intense labor made me feel anxious about my own pregnancy. I had little pain tolerance and could only imagine how this felt to a sixteen year old.

We walked back to the room. I helped her take off her slippers and hospital gown.

"Thank you, Shawnsy."

"You're welcome," I said, helping her into the standing shower.

"Do you want me to hose you down?" I teased her.

She nodded and smiled.

I adjusted the water and took the portable nozzle off the wall. Vicky held on to the bars while I playfully sprayed her naked body down like a dog.

Vicky smiled and I could tell it was helping her feel better, if only for a few minutes. The hospital towel was soft and fluffy. I put it around her. Vicky slowly dried herself and shuffled back to her bed. I helped her adjust her hospital gown.

A skinny, beautiful young Asian doctor walked in. "Hi, I'm Dr. Alison Lee and you must be Vicky's mother." Her tone and bedside manner were merry, yet highly professional.

"No, I'm actually a friend of Vicky's," I answered. Vicky and I made eye contact and smiled at each other. "Her mother should be here shortly."

"Oh, Shawnsy, will you stay with me when she comes?" Vicky pleaded, while grabbing my arm.

"Of course," I said, secretly hoping that Vicky's mother wouldn't mind.

"How are you feeling, Vicky?" Dr. Lee asked.

"Fine," Vicky answered clearly in pain.

"I just need you to lie back. We are going to check to see how far dilated you are," the doctor said, while gently adjusting the hospital sheet over Vicky.

Vicky cried, "When can I get some drugs?"

"I promise, as soon as I am done examining you."

Vicky closed her eyes and held her composure while the doctor quickly administered the exam. "You are now 4 ½ centimeters. I will page our anesthesiologist, to give you an epidural so we can get you out of this pain."

The good doctor immediately paged the anesthesiologist, and within minutes he was at the door.

"Here he is, the most popular man in the hospital. Vicky, he is going to take real good care of you while I go check on some other patients," Dr. Lee promised her.

I was surprised to see a young man who appeared to be right out of medical school. He had big horn-rimmed glasses, a crooked smile, and a goofy manner, but nonetheless, we were so glad to see him.

"Hello, my name is Dr. Earl, but don't worry I'm not like the man on the TV show."

His humor was refreshing and he worked steadily, helping Vicky get into position so that he could administer the epidural into her. He adjusted the machine while Vicky lay back quietly, waiting anxiously for the drug to kick in.

"Thank you, Dr. Earl." I smiled at him. "I can see why you are the most popular man in the hospital."

"Sadly, this is the only place I'm popular." he chuckled. "In a few minutes, you will feel a lot more comfortable; this stuff kicks in pretty quickly."

"It's nice to meet you both. If you have any questions, just push the clicker on the side of your bed, and Dr. Lee should be back in a few minutes. Good luck to you, kiddo," he said, waving goodbye.

Vicky suddenly looked more relaxed.

"Can I get you anything, some ice chips, maybe?"

"I have my water. I'm starting to feel better. Thank you."

Suddenly, there was a knock on the door. It was Vicky's family. They looked prim and proper as expected, as if they had walked out of a Sears catalogue. Vicky's parents greeted me and both of them gave me a warm hug.

"How is my little angel doing?" Vicky's dad asked.

"I'm starting to feel a little better now that I have drugs in me."

Vicky's mother and sisters hovered over her.

"Oh, honey, you're going to be just fine," Vicky's mom said, holding her hand.

"I'm just going to step out for just a little bit, if you don't mind, Vicky?" I asked.

"That's fine, I'm not going anywhere."

I wanted Vicky to have some alone time with her parents. I decided to go check on Keisha and Amy, who were still waiting anxiously with Wendy in the waiting room. On my way, I ran into Alma.

Alma asked, "I was just on my way back to Vicky's room. How is she doing?"

"She seems to be feeling a whole lot better. They gave her an epidural and she's a lot more relaxed. Her parents and sisters just arrived, so hopefully she'll have that baby soon," I explained.

"I'm glad her parents are here. Is it to be understood at this point that all the plans are set, and Vicky is going to return home with the baby?" Alma inquired.

"I guess that's the plan."

"Everything will work out just fine, unlike most of the girls I see. Vicky comes from a good home, and has a strong support system behind her," Alma said.

Alma and I were finally alone without the girls or any outside interruptions. I knew this was probably the best time to reveal my news. Even though I looked up to Alma as a strong, wise older woman, I couldn't help but feel somewhat intimidated by her. I wasn't sure how she would react to my news, and I was scared to death of telling her.

"Alma, I know you have been here awhile. Could I interest you in a cup of coffee?"

"That sounds really good; I certainly could use a cup."

We followed the signs to the café. It was not the usual sterile hospital cafeteria one would expect, it was more like a French coffeehouse with flavored coffees and lattés, gourmet sandwiches and salads, and a large glass case in front featuring an assortment of croissants, muffins and scones. I insisted to Alma it was my treat, and we both ordered a regular coffee and a butter croissant.

The café was empty, except for a couple of nurses sitting up front. I led Alma to a small table in the back corner.

"Thank you so much, Shawnsy, this is exactly what I needed," Alma said, while breaking apart her croissant.

"You are welcome. This is a really nice café. I would come to this hospital just for the café."

"I have to tell you, Keisha and Amy are so appreciative of the gowns you bought them. They told me how beautiful they are. That was very special of you to do that," Alma said, while slowly sipping her coffee.

"It was truly my pleasure. They deserve to feel beautiful. They have been through so much, and I thank you for giving me permission to do that."

"That was no problem. I hardly ever turn down an outing, and I certainly wouldn't for beautiful gowns from Ursula's, although they may be the most envied girls at the moving-up ceremony. But Keisha is our valedictorian for the year, so she should look beautiful and be envied, and it would be nice to see Amy looking lady-like for a change."

"They are going to be beautiful, and I would love to have their hair and makeup done that day, if you don't mind?"

"Why not, but I might want to be included too," Alma said with a big smile. "All of the girls on campus are going to request to live at the House of Love. You certainly do spoil them."

"Alma, there's actually something I need to speak to you about."

"What's going on, Shawnsy?" Alma asked seriously, putting her coffee cup down and leaning closer into me.

"I feel so uncomfortable talking to you about this, but I'm pregnant."

There was an awkward silence. Alma picked up her coffee cup and took a sip, as if she were at a loss for words.

"Shawnsy, I really don't know what to say. How are you feeling about all of this?"

"Believe it or not, I feel good and I am actually dealing quite well with everything. Detective McDermott is the father and we plan on getting married real soon," I said, feeling like a teenage girl defending myself.

"I suspected he was the father. Do the girls know about this?"

"They don't, because I wanted to discuss it with you first."

"My dear, you are a grown woman and that's all that counts. It's normally frowned upon when colleagues engage in a relationship. I had a feeling you and Detective McDermott were seeing each other. I'm a little disappointed that neither one of you came to me sooner about your relationship."

"I honestly didn't expect this to happen. I just came out of a marriage and I was told I couldn't have children. So falling in love and getting pregnant was something I least expected."

"Oh, you never know what life may bring. You're a very sweet girl, and of course, Detective McDermott is a charming fellow. I just hope you both didn't jump too fast into things."

"We really do love each other, Alma."

"If that's the case, then I wish you both the best," Alma said, her tone lightening up. "So how far along are you?"

"I am just going into my second trimester."

"How is everything progressing?"

"Everything is fine so far."

"How are you feeling?"

"I'm actually feeling pretty good."

"What are your plans once this baby is born?"

"Eric and I really are going to get married, nothing fancy, and hopefully it will be in the next few months. We will be living at my place at first, and our plan is to buy something else. But I have to talk to you about my job." I started to feel tense again. "I absolutely love working at St. Agnes' Place, but I don't think I can keep this crazy kind of schedule once I have the baby."

Alma looked at me kindly and said, "I would hate to lose you. Maybe we can work something out. You may not be able to work at the House of Love, but maybe I can arrange for you to have more stable hours somewhere else on campus if you decide you still want to work once the baby is born."

"I appreciate that, Alma," I said smiling softly at her. "When would you like me to tell everyone I'm pregnant?"

"I'll leave that up to you, but you have to promise me something?"

"What's that?"

"Please choose this place for your delivery. This is the best cup of coffee I have ever had."

"I promise," I said, grateful that we ended our talk on a good note.

"Give Vicky my best. I wish I could stay, but I have to head back. I have lots to do back on campus," Alma said, heading out the door.

"Alma!" I yelled before she went any further. "I really want to thank you for everything."

Alma turned around and smiled back at me. "You just take good care of yourself, Shawnsy. By the way, you are going to be having a new girl joining you at the house. And be prepared, we're going to get an awful rain later," Alma said obscurely, taking off in a scurry.

****

Another new girl to get used to, I thought to myself. Keisha, Amy, Vicky and I were our own makeshift little family, with the presence of Leelee always there. Hopefully, the girls and I will bond with her like a brand new puppy.

I entered the waiting room; Wendy, Keisha and Amy were nowhere to be found. I wondered if Wendy had lost all patience and brought them back to St. Agnes' Place. I walked back to Vicky's room, hoping her family had taken her mind off my absence.

I walked in to her room. Dr. Lee was standing at the foot of her bed, while Vicky's family and Wendy, Keisha and Amy stood guarding her on both sides.

"Shawnsy, you're back! Where were you? The doctor says I'm going to start pushing soon!"

"I ran into Alma and we started talking. I figured your mom was here. Alma sends her best but she had some things that had to be taken care of back on campus," I said, standing across the bed from Vicky's mother. She had one of Vicky's hands and I grabbed the other. Vicky was sweating profusely and was clearly in great pain as her contractions increased.

A nurse appeared, and prepped the delivery station.

"Is everyone staying in here for the delivery?" she asked, surveying the large group of us.

Keisha said, "I think I want to head out. I have a queasy stomach when it comes to stuff like this."

"Me, too," Amy agreed.

"That's fine, you guys," Vicky whimpered.

"I'll bring the ladies back to the waiting room. We'll be praying for you, Vicky," Wendy said, rubbing her leg.

I bent down toward the side of the bed and whispered in Vicky's ear, "Vicky, I think it's best your mother has you all to herself right now. I love you, and your mother loves you very much. Let her be the one by your side," I said, gently kissing her cheek.

Vicky nodded her head in agreement.

"All of us will be out there anxiously waiting for you and your little one," I said.

Vicky smiled at all of us through her pain.

"I love you, honey," Vicky's dad said, blowing her a kiss and leaving the room with her two sisters.

"I love you too, Daddy."

"I will have a nurse come and get all of you after she delivers," Dr. Lee informed us.

We all headed to the break room. It was a joy to watch the girls make small talk with Vicky's sisters, while Wendy, Vicky's dad and I waited anxiously.

The nurse arrived at what seemed only minutes later.

"I just want to let you all know that Vicky delivered a beautiful, healthy baby girl."

"She had a girl! Can we go see her?" Amy asked.

"Unfortunately, I have to ask you all to sit tight for a little while. We have to clean her up and run some tests, and then she will be ready for visitors," the nurse explained.

Keisha and Amy seemed overjoyed; while Vicky's young sisters seemed oblivious to what was going on. Vicky's dad, although by nature merry and sweet, seemed to wear his emotions on his sleeve. From the look on his face, I read relief that his daughter was all right, but concern for what would happen next. These were the very same emotions I felt, and assumed Wendy felt as well.

"I am going to get a drink at the water fountain," I said, as Keisha and Amy kept themselves busy playing with the little girls' hair and asking them silly questions about SpongeBob while Wendy and Vicky's dad made small talk.

I walked unnoticed over to Vicky's room. I peered through the narrow glass on the door. It was a bittersweet scene, watching Vicky rock her new baby girl, staring proudly into her eyes, as Vicky's mom lay by her side, smiling, with her arms wrapped around them both.

Chapter 18

I sat rocking gently in the chair usually occupied by Vicky. I missed her, but knew she would be back in a week to attend the moving-up ceremony, pick up more of her belongings, and show off her new little bundle of joy. I prayed that she was adjusting well to motherhood and moving back in with her parents. I started to flip through one of Vicky's pregnancy books she had left on the coffee table, when all of a sudden Keisha and Amy meandered through the door.

"Hey, Shawnsy, what's up?" Amy asked, almost out of breath.

"Nothing much. Did you get some good books?"

"I got a few good ones," Amy said, putting the books on the coffee table.

"I beat Amy racing back here," Keisha panted.

"You said 'go' after you started running," Amy said, defending herself.

"Oh, you're just a sore loser."

"What made you two race?"

"We just felt like it, and it looked like it was going to pour any second," Amy answered.

"Why don't you two have a seat and catch your breath. There is something I need to talk to you about."

"What's up?" Keisha asked, as she and Amy got comfortable on the couch.

"I just want to let you two know…I'm pregnant."

"Wow," Keisha said surprised, while Amy started laughing. Keisha nudged her, looking at a loss for words.

"So, who's the baby's daddy?" Amy asked.

"I'm sure you two have suspected that Detective McDermott and I have been seeing each other. He just so happens to be the father," I said my voice lowering with each word.

"Yeah, we knew you two were an item," Amy said with a sly smile.

"How far along are you?" Keisha asked.

"I'm about four months. I didn't tell Vicky yet. I figured I would tell her at graduation, but I did let Alma know."

"Oh my God, what did Alma say?" Amy asked.

"She was very supportive," I said, making Alma's response sound better than it actually was.

"That's good," Amy said.

There was a sharp knock at the door. I looked through the peephole. It was Alma.

"It's Alma," I announced.

Keisha and Amy let out nervous giggles.

"Hello, ladies, I thought I would pay you a visit," Alma said, removing a plastic rain bonnet revealing her gray bouffant hair and putting down her oversized umbrella.

"You can do some damage with that thing," Amy teased Alma.

"I may just have to," Alma said. "Actually, I am here to welcome a new friend to the house. I just got off the phone with Detective McDermott, and they should be arriving any minute," Alma said, making herself comfortable between Amy and Keisha on the couch.

"Another girl, that's just what we need!" Amy exclaimed.

"She will be staying in Leelee's room," Alma said, ignoring Amy's attitude.

"Another personality we have to deal with, Shawnsy," Keisha said, looking over at me.

I was surprised Eric didn't call me and give me the heads-up. I was in no mood, physically or mentally, to deal with another personality. All I could do was look back at Keisha and smile.

Suddenly, the bright headlights of Eric's undercover car shone through the translucent curtains.

"Ladies, you stay in here while Shawnsy and I go and greet her," Alma said.

It was a dark, ominous night. Eric pulled up and from the porch I could see the image of something large and restless hopping around in the back seat of his car.

Alma and I walked over to the car.

"Hi, Detective McDermott, how are you doing?" Alma asked.

"Hmm—let me just say we got a real live wire on our hands," Eric said, gazing into the back seat.

"Hi, Eric," I said.

He looked exasperated. "Hi babe, good luck with this one. I think I will be hanging out with you for awhile."

I peered in the back seat as the young girl was kicking his seat in frustration.

"That may not be a bad idea."

Eric opened the back door of the car.

"Can you cool it with the kicking? This is a brand new car!" Eric asked, losing his cool.

"Fuck you," she said, continuing to pound away with her feet.

Without warning, all one hundred pounds of Alma reached into the backseat and pulled her abruptly by the arm. "Come, my dear child. We are going to welcome you to your new home."

The girl did not resist. The dark mocha skinned girl was uncomely and incredibly overweight, with bulging big black eyes. She had short frizzy hair, pushed back by a blue headband. She slowly walked arm in arm with Alma up the front steps, while Eric removed her bags.

As we walked in the front door, Keisha and Amy were sitting at attention, waiting for the new arrival.

The angry girl slumped in the corner chair.

"I want to introduce you to your new housemates. This is Keisha and this is Amy," Alma said, patting each girl's head. They both responded with a shy "hi." And this is Shawnsy. If you have any needs, she is here for you, as well as myself. My name is Alma. I am the headmistress of St. Agnes' Place, and this is the House of Love. I hope you find your time here rewarding. Why don't you introduce yourself, and tell us a little bit about yourself?"

The girl looked defeated. With hurt in her eyes, she introduced herself as Rain and told us that she was sixteen years old and that she was from the city, and that she really had no choice but to come here, because it was either here or be placed in juvie.

"How did you get into the life?" Keisha asked.

Rain stared straight ahead, speaking as if in a trance. "I was lured into it by some twenty-something year old who gave me attention, bought me food and nice clothes. He told me he'd be my Daddy. He kept telling me how pretty I was, which nobody ever told me before. He got me hooked on him and drugs, and he made me feel like I had to do everything for him. And, so it began."

"We all know what you went through, Rain. We are all like you," Keisha said.

I knelt in front of her, putting my hands over hers. "Can I get you anything Rain—a drink or something to eat?"

"I'll have something to drink."

"We have some apple juice. Will that do?"

"That's fine."

Eric followed me out to the kitchen. "You are going to have to have a little more patience with this one. She's up and down."

"I feel bad for her."

"She'll be fine," Eric said, rubbing my shoulder. "But most importantly, how are you feeling?"

"Good, but tired," I responded, stroking his hair back. "You didn't feel awkward around Alma, did you?"

"Please. No one can make me nervous, not even Alma. I'm glad you told her, though."

"Thanks for giving me all the dirty work," I said, punching him in the arm.

I poured Rain a glass of juice and brought it out to her. Rain took a few sips and put it aside. She sat back motionless.

"Keisha and Amy, why don't you help Rain carry her bags up, and show her where the clean linen is? And, the two of you can even help her make her bed."

"We would love to, Shawnsy," Amy said, shooting me a look as she made her way up the stairs.

"You'll like your room. It's the biggest one in the house," Keisha said.

Rain followed them up the stairs in a zombie-like trance.

Alma, Eric and I sat down together in the living room.

In a quiet tone, Alma said, "I spoke with some of the counselors at Rain's rehab. She has supposedly been clean for about four months. She will continue with aftercare here.

She's young, scared, angry and broken. Hopefully, we'll be able to put her back together again."

"I think you may have better luck with Humpty Dumpty," Eric said.

I shook my head and rolled my eyes at Eric.

"We will certainly do our best with her. As you know, many girls act out when they first arrive here. I can assure you that in a few days she will be fine," Alma said.

Moments later, Keisha and Amy strolled down the stairs. "Rain just wants to stay in her room," Keisha said.

"She's probably exhausted," I answered.

"Can we watch some movies like we planned?" Keisha asked.

"That sounds like a nice evening for all of you. I am going to leave now. I'm sure you are fine with Detective McDermott watching over you. If you need me, you know where to find me. Ladies, please be patient with Rain; remember how it felt when you first arrived here. By the way, I hear congratulations are in order, Detective. I am sure you will make an excellent father," Alma said, adjusting her rain bonnet and grabbing her umbrella as she walked out the door.

"Thank you Alma, that means a lot."

"Bye, Miss Alma, we'll be good. I promise," Amy said.

"Bye, Alma," Keisha yelled.

I followed Alma out the door. "I have some extra clothes put aside here. Do you mind if I stay the night? The girls want to stay up late and watch movies, and I want to be here if Rain should wake up during the night."

"Suit yourself! I was actually going to peek in during the middle of the night. If you want to stay overnight, that's more than fine with me. Have fun, Shawnsy," Alma said opening her umbrella as some light rain began to fall.

"We'll try," I said.

I opened the door and smelled popcorn popping. It was nauseating. I walked to the kitchen where Eric was getting their drinks. I edged over to him, and gave him a quick hug. "I'm going to stay here for the night," I said, helping him with the drinks and popcorn.

"That's a good idea. I don't want you driving in this weather. I heard over my radio that there was a tornado warning."

"Are you going to stay a while and keep us safe?"

"Why not? I'm done with my shift and it's the only way I can see you."

"Oh, good!" I said, as we walked together into the living room.

"We put him to work, Shawnsy," Keisha said, as she and Amy mulled over the DVDs spread across the living room floor.

"Good for you! It's good for a man to become comfortable in the kitchen. I think I better go check on Rain, while the two of you pick out a movie."

I peeked through the curtains before I made my way up the stairs. It looked like the gray sky was going to rip open at any second. "Keisha, do you mind getting the candles ready? It's not looking so good out there."

"No problem and maybe we should choose a horror flick." Keisha grimaced, making a stabbing motion as she walked towards the kitchen.

Suddenly, a thunderous boom shook the house as rain poured from the sky. Keisha and Amy both let out ear-piercing squeals.

"Now, that is some heavy rain!" Eric exclaimed.

"It doesn't sound very good," I said, as I walked up the stairs. I knocked on Rain's door. There was no answer, so I gently opened it. Rain was rocking back and forth in bed with her hands covering her ears, chanting, "Rain, Rain, go away, come back some other day. If you don't, I don't care, because I'll pull down your underwear. I'll just pull down your underwear."

Chapter 19

I was unfortunately awakened from the very few hours of peaceful sleep I managed to get by the early morning sun, which shone brightly through the curtains. Staying up late with Keisha and Amy was a blast, even if it had been the twentieth time we had watched *Twilight*. I stretched and couldn't help but moan as I took off my warm covers. If I hadn't had the immediate urge to pee, I would have continued to stay wrapped up in a warm fetal position. I heard my phone vibrate from the side table. It was Eric texting that he was going to stop for doughnuts and come over. It sounded wonderful and I texted him back, reminding him that a very large coffee would be nice as well. I quickly used the bathroom and returned to my comfortable cocoon. Within minutes, Keisha and Amy were pounding their way down the stairs as Rain followed behind, marching to her own beat. The girls were still dressed in their mismatched sweat suits, while Rain still sported the barely fitting jeans and flannel top that she had fallen asleep in.

"Good morning," I greeted them, yawning widely.

Barely audible good morning moans emerged from all of them. Keisha curled up in the corner chair, while Amy sat on the floor below her. *True Life* was on MTV, and Amy and Keisha gave sideline commentaries on the young men and women who where battling gambling addictions in this particular episode. Rain, barely fitting in the rocking chair, leaned forward and stared, half-dazed, at the screen.

I announced to them that Eric was on his way with some doughnuts, and Amy let out a loud yoo-hoo.

Keisha said, "That means we can stay in our jammies all afternoon."

Rain asked, as she surfaced from semi-consciousness, "What do you guys do for fun on a Saturday afternoon 'round here?"

Amy remarked, "It depends on who's working that day. If it's Shawnsy, maybe a picnic or a new dress, if it's Wendy, then it's a whole different story."

"Who's on today?" Rain asked.

Amy looked over at me for confirmation. "Miss Wendy is on for the day. She'll be here in a few hours, right, Shawnsy?"

"That is correct. Rain, you'll love Wendy. She is very upbeat, unless these two are driving her crazy," I said, pointing to both Amy and Keisha.

Rain looked at me with a subtle smile. "These two girls be causing mischief 'round here?"

"Yes, Rain. I know it's probably hard to believe."

"Don't be causing trouble, Shawnsy," Keisha said, losing interest in her show.

Keisha leaned toward Rain, stared at her inquisitively and asked, "Rain, how 'bout I braid your hair?"

"You want to do my hair? Be my guest," Rain said as she pulled at the top of her hair. "Where do you want to do it?"

"Take a seat on the floor while I go get my comb," Keisha said as she got up and ran up the stairs.

Rain slowly maneuvered herself on the floor, which was funny to watch. Both Rain and Amy started laughing.

"You need some help there, girl?" Amy asked, clicking through the stations.

"I need lots of help!"

Keisha returned with her fine-toothed comb and immediately pulled back the top of Rain's hair.

Rain asked, "Are there going to be more girls living here?"

"Hopefully not, our friend Vicky just returned home, but she'll be back for the moving-up ceremony," Keisha said while swiftly intertwining Rain's hair.

"She went back with her family?" Rain asked.

"She did, because she had a baby," Keisha answered.

"Wow, she was pregnant!"

"And— guess what? Shawnsy's pregnant, too!" Amy blurted out.

"Damn, what you got going in the water 'round here? I'll be sticking with the apple juice." Rain chuckled.

"Yes, that's right. I'm pregnant," I said shooting Amy a dirty look as I watched, fascinated at the speed with which Keisha's fingers moved.

"We also had another girl here too; our friend, Leelee. You're in her old bedroom," Amy volunteered.

"Where she at now?" Rain asked.

"Don't ask," Keisha answered.

All of a sudden, a loud knock was heard at the door. All I could think was *thank God I can finally have some coffee.*

Amy quickly jumped up and opened the door for Eric.

"Speak of the devil, what took you so long with our doughnuts?" Amy asked Eric while opening up the box and grabbing a doughnut.

"Be nice, or I'll send you to the cafeteria so you can eat those donated muffin tops."

"Miss Rain, look at you getting all pretty. Knock any doors down lately?"

Rain shook her head and smiled at him.

"Keep your head still," Keisha said, holding her head in place.

"You know Detective McDermott is Shawnsy's baby's daddy," Amy said.

"You're kidding!"

"You have such a way with words, kiddo," Eric said, opening the box for me and putting the doughnuts on the side table. He made himself comfortable on the couch next to me.

"I really like how you put that, Amy," I said.

Amy just laughed and continued pressing buttons on the remote.

"How are you feeling, princess?" Eric asked.

"I'm still so tired. I'm not even going to shower until I get home," I said through bites of my doughnut.

"When you leave here, go home and relax," Eric said as he got up and grabbed the remote out of Amy's hand.

Amy said, "Hey, I am the controller of the remote. And, where are the doughnuts?"

"No, I am the controller of both the remote and the doughnuts. Maybe if you ask nicely, you can have another one."

"May I have another doughnut, please, Detective McDermott?"

Eric opened up the box next to him and handed Amy a white powdered sugar doughnut.

"No, no, no! That one shouldn't even have made it to the box. I'll have a Boston Crème, please."

"Because you said "please," here you go," Eric said, handing her the doughnut.

Amy grabbed it and settled herself on the floor.

Keisha continued to work away, pulling her fine-toothed comb through the bottom of Rain's coarse black hair.

"Girl, what the hell kind of tattoo you got going on here?" Keisha asked, pulling up the frizzy bottom of Rain's hair to expose a tattoo of numbers and a bar code.

Amy jumped up to view the peculiar tattoo. "That shit is wack!"

"I know it is, but it was put on me. I had no choice. I'm going to have it removed one of these days."

"Rain, do you mind if Shawnsy and I come over and look at it?" Eric asked.

"I don't mind at all."

We got off the couch with our hot coffees. Keisha held Rain's hair up at the nape of her neck. Amy continued to stand in back of her along with Eric and me. The tattoo was like nothing I had ever seen. It looked like some sort of cattle brand.

"Candyman put that on you, didn't he Rain?" Eric asked softly.

"Yes, he did. He's the one who turned me out."

"I don't get it. What does it mean? I asked.

"This particular type of tattoo is the pimp's way of marking them as his territory. It also makes the other pimps stay away, and tells the victim, "I own you, and I own you forever," Eric explained.

I was in shock.

"Damn," Keisha said, putting her other hand on top of Rain's head. She looked as disgusted as I felt.

"I'm sure someday you can get that removed," I said.

"My department is actually in the process of starting a program that will provide free laser removal for this type of stuff, because we are starting to see it more and more."

"I hope so, because it just always reminds me of the abuse."

"I'm so sorry, Rain," I said.

Amy, trying to lighten the moment said, "Rain, maybe someday Shawnsy can take us and we'll get a cool tattoo to cover it. In the meantime, we should do an experiment. We can all try lifting you up at the express checkout at Shop and Save and see if you ring up."

Rain started giggling, and suddenly I think we all had a visual of it because we all started laughing.

Chapter 20

"Seriously Eric, I have never heard of this before. It sounds nuts," I said eagerly as we left the doctor's office.

"You need to get with the program, Oprah," Eric said, shaking the small white envelope.

"This is the newest thing," Eric said, emulating a girly voice.

"Let me get this straight. You're going to go to the cake shop, hand them this top secret envelope, and request that a cake be baked. The inside will surprise us with whether it is a boy or a girl?"

"That's correct."

"And how are they going to make the inside of the cake blue or pink?"

"With food coloring, girl. Don't you watch Food Network?" Eric asked putting his hand on his hip and shaking his head.

"Hmm, very interesting."

"I know you want to know," Eric said, as he opened the car door for me.

"I do, but I don't. But I know you want to know."

"I kind of do, because I want to mentally prepare myself if it's a girl."

"Oh, because of what you deal with?"

"No because girls are one big giant pain in the ass!"

"Oh, that's not true. But, I must admit it does sound like a fun idea. There are no clues on the outside?"

"No, whatever design you choose is done in an array of colors."

"Wow, you are starting to scare me a little. How did you hear about this?"

"A few months ago, the wife of one of the guys in our department was going to have a baby, and she and her girlfriends got together and did this."

"And he told you about it?"

"Yes, we discussed it."

"I find that even more scary," I said as we got into the car.

"I must say, Shawnsy, I found it very intriguing," he said, rolling his eyes and pursing his lips.

"If you really want to do it, I just received word that Vicky is going to be visiting in a few days with her mom and baby. Maybe we can have a little get-together. I can tell them I'm pregnant, and then we can all eat cake."

"I thought Vicky was just coming back for the moving-up ceremony?"

"I ran into Alma yesterday, and apparently they are coming this Saturday. So, if you really want, you can get the cake for this Saturday."

"Oh, so you want me to take care of it?" Eric asked.

"It was your idea, and if you want to find out, you can get the cake."

"Only if I can get it at Coccadotts, and if I'm invited?" Eric asked, while finally starting the car.

"The cake must definitely come from Coccadotts. Their cakes are so good! But I don't know it might be a "Girl's Only" event."

"That's not happening, sweetheart. When I drop off the cake, I'm staying. Remember, you and I have to eat the last two slices."

"I guess there's no use arguing with you, so it's a plan! And, no trying to peek through the envelope, or interrogating the baker," I said.

"I'll try my best."

"Eric, I can't believe we saw our baby!"

"We did. Come on, you're not going to start tearing up on me again, are you?" Eric asked, glancing over at me as we pulled away from the doctor's office.

"Okay, I'll try not to."

****

Saturday came quicker than expected, and all day there was a feeling of high energy throughout the house. All of us were excited to see Vicky again and meet her baby. The girls had no idea about the cake or its significance. Eric arrived with a cocky grin on his face, dashing straight to the kitchen with the colorful sheet cake frosted in shades of purple, pink, yellow and blue. A stork holding a bundle of joy was on the top.

"Hey, babe," I greeted Eric with a kiss on the cheek. "The truth, you have no idea what's on the inside?"

"No, really, I don't."

"I'm having a hard time believing you! But, it looks delicious. I can't wait to find out what's inside," I said, taking the cake from him and putting it in the fridge.

"Where is everyone?"

"The girls are at an assembly with Alma and all of them should be here anytime now. Vicky and her mom should be arriving at any moment."

Eric said, pulling me closer to him, "I really don't think you are going to have to tell them you're pregnant.

They'll take one look at you and see you got a little belly going on."

"I know! It seems like in the past month I've put on about ten pounds. My wardrobe now consists entirely of maternity clothes."

"I know, but look at that glow," Eric said, squeezing my cheeks in an attempt to be funny.

We heard the sound of a car pulling up. I walked over to the window to see Vicky's mom sliding open the door of her suburban minivan for Vicky, who was unfastening the car seat. Eric joined me as I opened the door and greeted them. Vicky looked as if she had already lost all of her baby weight, but I noticed a spark missing from her as she walked up the path.

"Oh my, gosh, she is so beautiful," I said to Vicky as she held the sleeping baby close to her chest.

"Oh, thank you," Vicky said, leaning over to give me a kiss.

"Hi, Detective McDermott, how are you?" Vicky asked, surprised by his presence.

"I'm doing good, now what's the name of this little angel?"

"This is my little girl, Crystal Faith."

"She's a beauty."

"Thank you."

"Hey there, peanut," Eric said in a playful voice, bending close to the baby.

"That really is such a beautiful name, Vicky," I said, rubbing the baby's back.

"How are you doing?" I asked Vicky's mom.

"I'm hanging in there," she answered, giving me a slight hug.

"Come on in. The girls will be back soon. They are at an assembly with Alma. Can I get you something to drink?"

"Oh, no thank you," Vicky's mom answered, taking a seat on the couch.

"I'll get myself something in a little bit, after I get settled," Vicky said, positioning herself in the rocking chair as the baby awakened.

"I'll be back. I just have to return some calls," Eric announced, while reading some texts as he walked out the door.

"See you later," I called over to him.

Vicky's mom said, "Goodbye."

Vicky said "Bye" as she retrieved a bottle from the diaper bag.

"Can I feed her?" I asked.

"Sure," Vicky answered as she got up and placed the fidgety baby wrapped in a pink knitted blanket in my arms. "She's a little cranky when she first gets up."

"That just means she's hungry, Vicky. Do you have a burp cloth for her?" Vicky's mom asked.

"I'll get it," Vicky answered as she grabbed the diaper bag.

The beautiful baby girl had a light baby oil fragrance and her skin felt soft as I gently rubbed her cheeks and looked into her crystal blue eyes. Her eyes met mine with deep intimacy as she sucked at her bottle. Every bit of her was feminine–she was adorned with a white headband with a pink tiny ribbon in the center which covered her very fine golden hair. Her pink corduroy jumpsuit pulled up to her knees as she kicked, exposing her white socks with pink ruffles at the top.

Vicky handed me the burp cloth and I put it over my shoulder. After a few minutes, I gently held her over my shoulder and patted her back. She let out a surprisingly large belch that made all of us giggle.

"You are a natural at this, Shawnsy," Vicky's mom commented.

"I'm glad you think so," I said not wanting to let go of her. I held her face close to mine and made funny faces. She squealed back with delight. Then in an instant, her eyes squinted and she let out a piercing wail, which really made her look even more adorable.

"I think she wants her mommy back. Or is it you don't like my funny faces?" I asked her in a baby voice.

Vicky came over and gently took her. "Shawnsy, there is something we want to talk to you about. Mom, do you want to tell her, or should I?"

"Honey, you can go ahead."

I sat anxiously, waiting for them to say what they had to say. I wanted to share the news of my pregnancy as well.

"How do I begin? The past few weeks have been pretty intense in our house, with me adjusting to being back. My parents, sisters and I have been getting along really great, so it's nothing like that. It's just that I'm still trying to get myself right. I thought I had gotten myself together while I was here, but I realize I really didn't, and I think it's going to take some time," Vicky said, pausing to catch her breath. "I love my baby girl more than anything, but I'm not ready emotionally to care for her, and my mom and dad have their hands full with my baby sisters. It may sound selfish, but I just want to have some of my own life back before I become a mother."

I glanced at Vicky's mom, who had tears in her eyes. I was in shock at what I thought she may be implying.

"Vicky, do you think maybe you are just experiencing some post-partum depression? Many women feel this way after having a baby."

"Shawnsy, I know what post-partum depression is. It's not that. I'm just not ready for all of this."

"What do you think of all of this?" I asked, looking over at Vicky's mother.

"My husband and I finally agree that it's not fair to have Vicky keep her daughter. We realize we can never raise Crystal Faith because we really need to concentrate on making sure Vicky stays well," Vicky's mom said through her tears. "Shawnsy, there's something Vicky and I would like to ask you."

All of a sudden, we were interrupted by the roaring jabber of the girls tramping up the porch, with Eric trailing behind them. Like a heard of elephants, they entered the room and immediately swarmed around Vicky and her baby.

"Is it cake time, yet?" Eric asked loudly over the roar of oohs and aahs.

"Eric, can you come into the kitchen with me for a minute?"

"I just need to excuse myself for one moment," I said to Vicky and her mother.

Eric followed me out to the kitchen.

"Listen, I need to talk with Vicky and her mom privately for a few minutes."

"Can we just cut the cake first?" Eric asked rubbing his hands together.

"No, I didn't have a chance to tell her I'm pregnant yet," I said quietly.

"What's the big deal? I think she has probably guessed by now."

"I can't explain right now, but I'm going to ask Vicky and her mom to step outside with me for a few minutes. Can you hang tight with the girls for just a bit?"

"Fine, but make it quick," Eric said pretending to hit a golf ball. I kissed him on the cheek and went nervously out to the living room.

"Girls, I don't mean to break up your party." As I spoke, they all turned around and looked at me. "Detective McDermott was kind enough to bring us a cake. If you wouldn't mind, can you get the plates, forks and drinks ready?"

The girls all looked pleasantly surprised.

"We're having cake. What's the occasion?" Vicky asked.

"I'll tell you and your mom about it outside," I said patting Vicky's shoulder.

Vicky's mother followed Vicky and her baby and me out to the porch. Vicky and I took a seat on the glider rocker, while her mom sat across from us on a rocking chair.

"What's going on? Is the cake for that new girl? What's her name?" Vicky asked.

"No, the cake is not for her. Her name is Rain and she just arrived last week. What I wanted to tell you and your mom is that Detective McDermott and I are expecting a baby."

"Oh," Vicky's mom said.

Vicky sat shocked. "Shawnsy, my mom and I were going to talk to you about adopting. My mom and I thought you would make a perfect mother for Crystal Faith."

I was stunned and at a loss for words. I put my arm around Vicky as we rocked together on the glider rocker. I was full of emotion.

"Oh, Vicky, I love you and I can't help loving your baby girl," I said, rubbing my hand down Crystal Faith's soft skin. She is so beautiful. I would love to make her part of our family. I would need to talk to Eric, of course. But, would you still consider me for her mother and Eric for her father?"

"Shawnsy, Detective McDermott rescued me, and I couldn't think of a better man to raise my baby. But Shawnsy, you're now expecting your own child. Why would you even want mine?"

"Vicky, this is everything and more than I ever wanted. Everything is so unexpected, but so beautiful. This is the life I always wanted."

Vicky moved closer to me, and put her head on my shoulders while we continued to rock. We were all silent for a moment, as we gathered our emotions.

Finally, Vicky broke the ice. "What, exactly, is the cake for again?"

"Oh my God, I forgot they're waiting for us," I said, getting up quickly and pulling on Vicky's sleeve.

As the three of us trudged through the door, we were welcomed by a chorus of nervous giggles.

Three slices were laid out on the dining room table with napkins covering them, while Eric and the girls stood to the side carefully, concealing the contents of their plates.

"I'm sorry, Shawnsy, we couldn't wait any longer," Eric said, handing me a slice of cake completely covered with frosting on all sides.

He leaped over to Vicky and her mom and gave them each a slice with a napkin on top of it. "Wait, don't eat it yet!" he said with his hand up.

Amy asked, "What do you think, Shawnsy; are you going to have a ballerina or a baseball player?"

"I'm confused," Vicky said, while her mom stood dumbfounded.

"You'll see, Vicky," Amy said, taking bites out of her cake.

Keisha yelled, "Come on Shawnsy, take a bite!"

"Shawnsy, take a bite!" Rain echoed.

I slowly dug my fork into the cake and looked up at all of them.

"I guess we are going to have a little Yankees fan on our hands," I said, overjoyed, putting the cake into my mouth.

Chapter 21

"Rain, throw me down a blue marker!" Amy yelled from the other side of the long dining room table.

The table was cluttered with used magazines, scissors, pencils, magic markers, crayons, and different colored poster board. The girls each had to complete an art project, depicting how they viewed their past, present or future. All of their art work would be displayed later that evening at the Washington Lake House during the Taking Back the Night Rally. I sat along with the girls, doodling stars and rainbows on a notepad, and coloring them in with crayons. I forgot how much fun I used to have coloring. It had been such a long time since I picked up a crayon; it brought back memories of sitting at my grandmother's kitchen table with my sister Gwen, coloring for hours in books she had bought especially for our visit.

"Ain't No Mountain High Enough," Amy said as she held up her finished project. The picture had three narrow brown mountains, with a sherbet looking sky, and a royal blue river below. On the bottom was the title of the famous song, and in small print, Amy scrolled her initials.

"I will explain," Amy said in a mock scholarly fashion, holding up her picture for all to see. "The mountains represent adversity which I have encountered and shall continue to overcome. The bright orange sky represents sunlight and positivity."

"Wow, Amy, that was deep," Keisha said, looking up from her project.

"Why, thank you, Keisha," Amy responded.

"Who aren't the mountains and rivers keeping you from?" Rain asked.

"It's a metaphor for nothing can stop me from achieving happiness. It's not about a man."

Keisha laughed and said, "You're starting to really freak me out, Amy."

"I know I'm good! What you got going on over there, Keisha?"

Keisha held up her almost finished picture. It was an amazing scene drawn in pencil of a bridge, and underneath it was wavy water with two hands about an inch apart, separated, except for the handcuffs holding them together.

"Bridge over Troubled Water," Keisha said.

"Girl, you're a deep thinker, and you can draw," Rain said.

"Keisha, you're an extraordinary artist," I said, amazed at the details in her work.

"What's it all mean, Keisha?" Amy asked.

"I tried to convey in this picture the struggles I still have with my mother because we are still locked together as a family, hence the handcuffs. The high tide of the troubled water represents the ups and downs in our lives."

"That's really good, Keisha," Amy said.

"It is unbelievable," I said, continuing to stare at it.

"Thank you," Keisha said.

Rain sat back and shook her bare paper. "Damn, you girls are making me look bad. I was just going to cut out pictures of some bling."

"What do you mean cut out pictures of some bling?" Keisha asked.

"I mean some fine jewelry."

Keisha asked, "What's that have to do with anything?"

"'Cause, that's what I want in my future. I see that as success."

"That's not success," Keisha said.

"To me it is!" Rain answered.

"That's also what got you into trouble," Keisha said.

"That ain't what got me into trouble."

"Then, what do you think did?" Keisha asked.

Amy let out a raucous laugh as she listened to their banter. I also was as curious as Keisha.

"Being forced into the life and getting hooked on drugs."

"I'm sure some sweet-talking brother with bling did all the forcing," Keisha said.

"You're probably right, and it was those rich white politicians that did all the buying."

Amy asked, smirking from across the table, "They liked you, Rain?"

"I was a whole lotta woman for them." Rain laughed and then we all laughed along with her.

"Aren't you angry, especially how men like that seem to get away with it?" Keisha asked.

"No because that's amazing grace. God has forgiven me, and although it wasn't fair the way I was used, I made a choice to forgive them."

"Rain, I think you have a theme for your artwork," Keisha said.

****

That evening all the women from the various houses at St. Agnes' Place met in the parking lot to board a bus to the rally. Alma stood up front and explained the history and importance of the rally that we were all about to take part in.

She explained how the movement gave not only women, but also men a forum to speak out and break the silence through art, dancing, acting, and poetry. Also many of the survivors would be sharing their testimonies. The girls held tight to their intimate works of art that were secured with rubber bands. Overpowering chants of "No Means No," and "On the Campus and on the Streets, We Won't Be Raped We Won't Be Beat" greeted us as we made our way off the bus. A twenty-something college girl with horn-rimmed glasses, a noticeably large eyebrow ring and slick black hair held tightly in a ponytail, wearing a blue t-shirt with the slogan, "I Love Consent" greeted all of us as we stood in front of the bus. She thanked all of us for coming, and informed us that our voices would be heard. She thanked each girl personally for their artwork which she referred to as testimonies of their strength, and said within the hour, the projects would be hung in the Lake House for all to see.

The night was cold and windy. Large colorful banners with moons and stars blew in the wind—banners with slogans such as "Sexual Violence Must Go" and "No More Profits Off Of Women's Bodies." Each of the houses of St. Agnes' Place went off on its own, while Alma walked among us. There was a strong energy in the air as we walked from booth to booth. The booths were staffed with women from the local crisis centers, and shelters, and college and university groups showcased their cause. Our girls were visibly happy, and all proudly wore the neon green glow necklaces, bracelets, and pins with words of empowerment with which they gifted us.

We made our way through the crowds and into the Lake House. The girls were excited to see their artwork displayed on easels when we first walked in.

"Check this out ladies. This here is my masterpiece!" Rain said.

To the surprise of all of us, it was a powerful work done in dark hues. Rain had drawn a thick diagonal chain torn apart in the center.

"Rain, this is amazing," Amy said.

"Rain, that is really very good," I said, patting her back.

"It's good, Rain, but what's it mean?" Keisha asked.

"It's what I call, "Amazing Grace." The chains are broken. I'm realizing now I don't have to be bound to heartache and bad people, and I know that things may not be fair, but I'll let Him do the judging."

We all stood silent in awe of the words Rain had spoken.

After a few seconds, Amy broke the silence by pointing to the large clothesline stretching from one end of the room to the other. "There are the t-shirts."

The t-shirts were decorated by women affected by violence and conveyed their painful emotions. At first, we stood together and looked at a few, and then we all drifted off in our own quiet solitude. The shirts stabbed at our hearts. Each shirt affected each of us in different ways. The words and actions which were mostly drawn in stick-figures were heart-wrenching. They were so intense to simply view, that I could only imagine how Rain, Amy, and Keisha felt, having had to endure this type of evil themselves.

In the corner of my eye, I saw Amy wiping her nose on her hoodie, which surprised me because of her usual lack of emotion. Rain and Keisha were out of my view, but I knew this was one time they needed to be alone and deal with their grief in their own way.

Suddenly, a loud voice was heard over the loud speaker announcing that it was time for the candlelight vigil and march to begin. I scanned the room to see where the girls were, and somehow with perfect timing, we all met in the front of the lake house. A manly-looking woman gave each of us a candle in a blue cup with a white star on it. A woman in the crowd lit Rain's candle, and Rain's candle provided the light for all of ours.

We followed the crowd as it walked along the lake onto the downtown streets of the city. The chant began slowly: "Hey-Ho, No-Means-No-We-Won't-Be-Bought-We-Won't-Be-Sold." As we made our way midtown through the city the chant built to a climax. This is when we all started reciting it in warrior fashion. A burst of emotion emerged from Amy as tears suddenly streamed down her face. Keisha put an arm around her and held her close as they marched side by side.

Chapter 22

"Are you sure you don't want to at least continue through the summer?" Alma asked as we walked through the courtyard.

The courtyard was filled with scattered sand, a reminder of last night's heavy rain showers. There was moisture in the air, and the humidity was beginning to become quite unbearable. The distant sounds of the orchestra rehearsing echoed throughout the campus along with the banging noise of tables and chairs being set up. The caterers worked diligently, unloading their trucks in preparation of the day's event.

"Their whole routine changes around here during the summer with all their day trips and summer events. This is a good time for Rain and Amy to get acclimated to me not being here. Keisha is leaving in a few months for her new school, and Vicky is gone. If I'm going to leave, this really is the best time. Wendy could really use the extra hours." I stopped and turned to face Alma. "But I want you to know, Alma, I am so grateful to you for giving me a chance to work here. St. Agnes' Place really changed my life. I thank you so much for everything, but I know I won't be able to handle being a working parent."

"Please, promise you will stop by and visit us occasionally?"

"Of course Alma, I promise I will stop by periodically to check on you, Wendy, Amy and Rain. I am going to miss all of you so much! I'm so used to all of you being such a huge part of my life. Each one of the girls and you will always have a special place in my heart. Alma, you are truly the matriarch and force behind St. Agnes' Place, and I'm especially going to miss you," I said, giving her a hug.

"Oh, Miss Stevens don't you go getting all emotional on me," Alma said, smiling. "I just pray your heart is at peace with the decision you and Detective McDermott are making."

"It's all Eric and I have been discussing for the past few weeks and we weighed all the factors and feel very confident in our decision," I said as we continued to walk again.

"I'm glad, and this place is starting to transform in front of our very eyes," Alma said, observing the many workers.

"And so will the girls once my friend Serena gets her hands on them. I have to go," I said, noticing the time on my watch. "Are you sure you don't want my friend to do your hair? She's incredible."

"I'm sure she will do a fabulous job on the girls, but it would take a Christmas miracle to transform this former nun," Alma said, pointing to herself. "I thank you for the offer, but I don't want anyone to go into shock during the ceremony."

"If you change your mind, you know where to find us," I said, hurrying back to the House of Love.

****

As I was walking up the path, I was met by my dear old friend, Serena. She was an effervescent, five-foot-eleven, raven-haired former model and owner of the famed Above and Beyond Spa and Resort in Saratoga Springs. She had become my friend, confidante and hairstylist when Jon was her attorney and won her millions in her divorce settlement against her wealthy husband, the former president of Saratoga's Racino.

"Hello, dear Shawnsy and baby!" Serena called from her car window, looking down at my stomach as she pulled up in her glossy, bright red Mustang.

I waved back, excited to see her. Serena was one of the few people who called me after my divorce to check on me. She said she knew the pain of being duped by a lawyer because she had been with a few of them in her day. It had been a while since I had seen Serena, and we had talked for more than an hour when I had called to make the girls' appointment. I had been letting my hair go since the pregnancy. Making the long drive out to Saratoga Springs on my day off for a haircut seemed a little extreme, even though she was the best hairdresser I had ever had. Serena wanted the full 411 on Eric, the girls, my pregnancy and my new life. I told her everything, and she said she would be honored and would love to come personally to the St. Agnes' Place to meet all the girls, and she would be thrilled to see me again. As she exited the car, she pulled off her designer sunglasses and gave me a kiss on both cheeks.

"You look radiant, darling," she said as she proceeded up the path to the House of Love as if she were walking the red carpet.

The house was ablaze with a commotion that one would find in Grand Central Station. Rain was parading around the living room, showing off her outfit. Keisha stood in the corner, facing the wall, rehearsing her speech.

Amy pleaded, "Shawnsy, please tell her she looks good. This is the third outfit she has tried on."

"I'm sorry, Amy, but the Charity House does not cater to us full-bodied women. My selections were limited," Rain explained.

"Rain, you look beautiful," I said.

Rain looked classy and quite conservative. She wore a sharp white ruffled shirt with a long, gleaming pearl necklace that stood out against her ebony skin and black pant suit. The outfit looked as if it had been donated by a fifty-something business woman. Although she was not eligible to participate in the ceremony, Alma made her feel important. Rain was given the role of greeting the guests and handing them a program. She was very excited about her part in the ceremony and proud that Alma took a special interest in her.

"Serena, these are the girls I spoke to you about. This is Rain and this is Amy, and in the corner is our very own Keisha, who will be leading the ceremony," I announced, pointing to each one of them. The girls all turned to say hello, and they all stood mesmerized by Serena's exotic good looks.

"Hello, ladies! Let's get this party started. I have a lot of work to do!"

Serena laid out her hair and beauty supplies on the dining room table like a surgeon getting ready to perform major surgery.

"Come, my fashion diva," Serena said, pointing to Rain.

With precision and speed, Serena performed a miracle on Rain. She gave Rain a sleek style by lightly applying gel to the front of her hair and brushing it to the side. She stroked raspberry colored blush up and down her cheekbones, and delicately applied light green eye shadow, giving her eyes a surprisingly soft appearance. She finished by applying a pink gloss on Rain's full lips.

Serena whipped her big hand held mirror off the table and held it in front of Rain. "You are a beautiful young woman, Rain," Serena said, leaning her head next to Rain's and staring in the mirror along with her.

"Thank you, I do look good," Rain said.

We all looked at Rain in awe as she took a place on the couch next to Amy.

"Rain, you look so beautiful," I said smiling at her. Rain confidently smiled back.

Amy jumped off the couch, with her hair pulled back in a ghetto-bun, insisting that she be next.

"My love, this must go, for good," Serena said, grabbing Amy's bun with great force.

"It's ghetto fabulous," Amy said.

"This isn't a style, it's a crime, and your hair is way too beautiful for it. I will give you a classy, elegant updo," Serena said, removing the bun, and gliding her long French-manicured nails through Amy's hair. She sleeked Amy's bangs to the side and took a heated iron and created loose curls through the back of her hair. She finished by pinning it up in the back. Amy looked like a princess.

Serena quickly put a foundation base over Amy's face, and light concealer under her eyes, and finished her off with copper eye shadow and brown liner, a pale pink blush, and coral lipstick.

We all simultaneously said, "Wow," as we looked at the transformed Amy.

Serena gave her the mirror and stood proudly next to her. "Is that really me?"

"It is you, darling. You have always been beautiful, you just needed to let it show," Serena said, sounding like Glinda, the good witch of the North.

"What can I say, I'm hot stuff!"

"And now for the master of the ceremony," Serena announced as Keisha proudly walked over to her.

"You are such a beautiful girl," Serena said, bending in front of her and pushing her fingers through Keisha's silky black hair.

"Thank you."

"I think we should show off your naturally long hair, with some loose curls. What do you think?" Serena asked, trying to put the visibly nervous Keisha at ease.

"That sounds good."

"What an honor you have been given. You must have worked very hard?" Serena asked running a comb through Keisha's hair.

"Yeah, I study a lot."

"You are going to do fabulous today, and look stunning as well," Serena said as she clamped the hot iron in Keisha's hair, creating long, loose shimmering curls.

Rain yelled, "You look like a rock star!"

"Keisha, you're looking really good," Amy added.

"Keisha, you look stunning," I said, not able to take my eyes off of her.

Keisha did not answer and sat with a nervous smile on her face.

"Now, for some light makeup, because that is all you really need," Serena said, accenting Keisha's green eyes with sage eyeshadow and light brown liner, her cheeks with light rose blush and her mouth with pale pink lipstick.

"You, my dear, are simply breathtaking," Serena said, holding the mirror in front of Keisha.

"I like it, thank you so much," Keisha said in shock.

"You are so welcome, my love, and good luck today," Serena said, looking at Keisha and admiring her work.

"Shawnsy, thank you so much for doing this for all of us," Keisha said.

"You're welcome," I said, elated that the girls were so happy.

"Thank you, Shawnsy, you're the best," Amy said.

"Thank you. You made me feel so beautiful," Rain said.

"It was my pleasure." I looked down and noticed the time.

"Girls, you better put your dresses on now. We don't have much time."

"It was nice meeting all of you," Serena said in her charming manner.

Keisha, Rain, and Amy each went over and thanked her and gave her a gentle hug, not wanting to disturb their transformation.

The girls rushed up the stairs.

"Now, what should we do for you?" Serena asked, looking at my hair intently.

"Oh, I didn't expect anything today."

"You must be sweating to death with all this hair?" she asked, messing it up.

"Lately, I just have been putting it up in a ponytail."

"The classic pregnancy do," Serena said, shaking her head disapprovingly.

"Have a seat," she said, taking out her scissors.

As if on a mission, she cut my hair with speed. Strands fell to the floor. I had no idea what she was up to, but I knew Serena knew best.

All at once, she stopped and walked in front of me to check that both sides of my hair were perfectly even. Without saying a word, Serena handed me the mirror.

I loved it. My dirty blonde hair was cut in a bob-longer length in the front and cropped shorter in the back.

"I really like this, Serena. It's a new me," I said, surprised at my reflection.

"Now you are in style," Serena said, as she began to wrap up her supplies.

The girls made their way down the stairs and they were a sight to behold.

Serena and I both commented how beautiful they looked. The girls were equally shocked to see me, and couldn't believe how different I looked.

"Girls, get close together. I need a picture for my website," Serena commanded while clicking buttons on her cell phone.

The three of them wrapped their arms around each other with Rain in the center. I took out my cell phone as well.

Serena yelled, "Say Cheese," and all of them smiled proudly. I stared at the picture on my phone. It was picture perfect.

Later that afternoon, all the girls at St. Agnes' Place met in front of the campus center and stood in a formal line as they had rehearsed the night before. With minutes to spare, Wendy arrived and finally, Vicky with her mom by her side. Vicky kissed her mom quickly goodbye. She looked radiant in a pale blue off-the-shoulder satin ball gown. She had on a sparkling rhinestone necklace and earrings. Her golden hair flowed to her shoulders in soft curls, and a corsage of pink and white carnations adorned her right wrist.

Alma stood in front of the parade of girls, with Keisha leading the pack. All of the girls at St. Agnes' Place looked their best, each with their own personal style. Rain and the two other selected greeters were ahead in the distance, handing out programs and welcoming all of the anxious guests. It was silent as all the girls stood at attention. I smiled at Vicky and signaled her to take her place in line.

Within minutes, a few chords from a cellist were heard. The crowd quieted as the rest of the quartet joined in and played two songs of soothing, tender music. After an awkward few seconds of silence, the band began to perform "Pomp and Circumstance" as the girls began their entrance. All the girls looked like beautiful butterflies as they proudly walked down the center aisle. The flash of cameras and the sounds of small children welcomed them on both sides.

Alma took the podium and welcomed the excited crowd. She spoke openly about the struggles many of the girls at St. Agnes' Place had to overcome, and about how her journey with them was at times troublesome, but that seeing them here today making a step in the right direction made it all worthwhile. She spoke wholeheartedly of how she loved each and every girl, and that St. Agnes' Place would always be a place they could call home. Alma then turned, and warmly welcomed the school's leader for the year in academics and achievement, our valedictorian, Miss Keisha Ardiss. The crowd clapped and roars from the girls cheered her on.

Keisha gracefully walked up to the podium, and with great ease and confidence, adjusted the microphone. She addressed the enthusiastic crowd, "I first want to thank Alma, and all of my teachers and counselors for all their guidance and support. If it weren't for them, I would never have realized that I had this potential within me."

With a sweet smile on her face she continued, "I also want to thank my two special house aides, Wendy and Shawnsy. The two of you have shown me such unconditional love and always made me feel safe and secure. And at times, you both really spoiled me."

Keisha let out a slight giggle. "To my longstanding housemates, Vicky and Amy, I thank you so much for putting up with me, and always putting me in my place, especially you, Amy. You two really have become like sisters I never had, and I love you both very much. And, Rain, my newest housemate, keep up the hard work. I promise it will pay off.

To my friend, Leelee, I miss you so much and I wish you were here today. You will always have a special place in my heart. But, I know you are dancing with the angels and smiling down on us.

Overall, I want to express that St. Agnes' Place has taught me freedom. Before coming to this school, I felt captive to the bad circumstances and poor choices that had dictated my past. I essentially felt broken, spiritually and emotionally. I was in my own prison of guilt and shame. I thought I would always be the person I was. But now I am finally free, and I realize I have value and am more than worthy of a healthy, abundant and beautiful life. In closing, I want to thank St. Agnes' Place for showing me how to take back my life. I truly do thank you."

As Keisha made her way back to her seat, I saw her turn around and look my way and smile. I gave her two thumbs up with tears in my eyes.

****

Everyone cheered as Alma announced the names of the rest of the girls. Each girl came up quickly and gladly received their certificate of merit. After everyone returned to their assigned seat, Alma thanked the crowd for being there to show their support. Each girl walked back through the aisle to await their family and friends as the band performed an upbeat jazz tempo. Wendy and I greeted Keisha and Amy with open arms as they made their way to the back of the courtyard.

"I am so proud of you," I said to Amy as I gave her a huge bear hug.

I turned to Keisha and put my hands on her face. "You, my dear, were amazing up there. You did a great job." We hugged each other tightly.

"I meant everything I said up there."

"I know you did," I said, hugging her again.

Wendy gave them each a hug and congratulations as well.

"Where's Vicky?" Wendy asked, looking around.

"She probably met up with her family," Amy said.

"We should go find her," I said, looking forward to seeing her.

"Can we go over there and get some punch and cookies first? I'm starving!" Amy asked, pointing to one of the many stations that were set up throughout the courtyard.

"I really need something to drink," Keisha said.

"You should. You gave quite a speech up there," Wendy said putting her arm around Keisha's shoulder.

We walked over to the skirted table. The girls started laughing as Amy tried to ladle the punch without spilling it.

All of a sudden, we heard a deep voice resonate in back of us.

"You gave a really nice speech up there, Keisha." Keisha turned around with a startled look on her face.

I was awed as well, as I remembered having met her on my surprise visit to the jail with Eric. She looked exactly the way she had when I first met her, except that her yellow jumpsuit was replaced with clean blue jeans and a royal blue cotton top.

"Mom, what are you doing here?"

"I was invited."

"I thought you were in jail?" Keisha asked.

"I'm out, and I'm living back at your grandmother's old home. I got a call telling me that you were going to be transferred in a few months, and they mentioned your graduation."

"Oh," Keisha answered, surprised and at a loss for words.

"Keisha, I came here to tell you I'm sorry and I want to do you right and be a part of your life. I want you to come back home with me, and let me take care of you for a while."

Keisha stared at her mother with a look of contempt. "You're telling me what you want to do for me. You're not capable. I've been through the past with you, and I know what I will see in the future, because it just keeps repeating."

"Will you at least give me another chance?"

Keisha shook her head in disgust and quickly turned and walked away. The three of us stood stunned, along with Keisha's mom, who just continued to stare at her fleeing daughter.

Out of nowhere, Rain came over like a bolt of lightning. "Hey girls, look! I got a gift card for the mall from Alma for being such a good greeter."

We all just looked over at her and ignored her.

"What's going on?" Rain asked.

Suddenly, Keisha turned around and walked slowly toward her mother. Both of them started crying as they fell into each other's arms. "Mom, I really do need you!"

Chapter 23

"I don't know how the two of you pulled this off, but this is exactly what Eric and I wanted," I said as I waddled over to Kristen and Michaelann. The three of us embraced in a big group hug.

"I'm not so sure this is what he wanted." Michaelann laughed, pointing to the upside down pig.

"Aww, come on, don't make me feel bad; it's my wedding day!"

"I know who had better get the first taste of porky pig," Kristen said, pointing to Angus Beef.

The large Rottweiler stood salivating with her eyes fixed on the hanging pig.

"She hasn't left its side since 6:00 this morning when Eric showed up with my brother and his partner," Kristen said.

Thanks to the pig, the whole outdoors had a smoky barbecue aroma that left me longing for a piece of the pig just as much as Angus Beef.

"Come here, Angie, get over here, girl," I said patting my knees in an attempt to pull her away.

The eager dog jumped up and down on her hind legs and glanced in my direction trying her best not to lose sight of the pig.

"I don't think I have to worry about her going anywhere today," I said.

The backyard at Michaelann's and Marty's home was transformed into a Hawaiian luau. Lighted palm trees towered in each corner of their deck. Directly below stood rows of chairs covered and decorated with white bows for the ceremony. Rented round tables with flowered umbrellas lined both sides of the sprawling estate for the reception. Each table was covered casually with a different brightly colored plastic tablecloth. Kamani wood tea light candles decorated the tables along with pineapple photo frame magnet favors for each of the guests.

"We better get you inside before Eric shows up and sees you. You know its bad luck to see your future spouse before the wedding," Kristen said, locking her arm in mine and leading me into the house.

"Does that rule apply to second marriages as well?" I asked.

Michaelann answered, "I don't think you should play around with Lady Luck."

Michaelann's daughter and Kristen's two daughters were busy in the dining room arranging baskets with sea-shell leis to hand to each of the guests upon arrival. The girls also volunteered to take pictures throughout the day. I couldn't believe how much they had grown. The years had quickly flown by, and they were now teenagers, almost the same age as many of the girls at St. Agnes' Place. I looked at the three of them and saw a charming innocence, and I wanted to tell them how fortunate they were to be unscathed by horrible people.

Kristen announced, "The girls have a gift for you."

Each of the girls smiled, as Kristen picked up the huge hat box on the table.

"I told you we would help you out, and I know this isn't a traditional wedding, and you said you were just going to wear a big fat white tent, instead of a wedding dress with a veil." Kristen laughed. "But, I saw this in a magazine, and I couldn't resist. Michaelann and all the girls helped me pick out all the flowers and put it together. I really hope you like it," she said, opening up the box.

I could smell a light, pleasant lilac scent as I pulled back the white tissue, and gently lifted out my surprise.

"Oh my gosh, this is so beautiful," I said, admiring the colorful array of lilacs, lilies, orchids and hibiscus."

"Go ahead, try it on," Michaelann said.

The beautiful crown fit snug on my head. They all loved it on me, and I couldn't wait to go get changed so I could see it for myself.

"Thank you so much. This really is absolutely beautiful," I said, taking it off and admiring it. "This is nicer than any veil I could ever have chosen."

"I thought it would blend well with the Hawaiian theme, and add a little something to your white sundress. By the way, it's called a "haku lei," and it could be used for your "something new,"" Kristen explained.

"I definitely love my haku lei. I can't wait to see it on me, but now I need something, "old, borrowed, and blue.""

Michaelann said, "You can borrow Marty for a little bit before the ceremony. He's old."

"Thanks for the offer!"

"I got it. I have a blue shell necklace that can count for "borrowed and blue,"" Michaelann offered.

Kristen said, "I think that's double-dipping!"

"It does sound nice, and these pearl earrings were my grandmother's," I said, touching my ears.

"I better start getting ready," I said, anxiously grabbing my haku lei.

"Do you want some help?" Kristen asked.

"Thank you, but it would be like trying to help a baby elephant. I'll be fine."

I quickly washed my face, brushed my teeth, and took off my comfy elastic waist-shorts and jumbo-sized shirt. I slid on my white off-the-shoulder maternity sundress that I had bought off a clearance rack at Target; a long stretch from Ursula's where I originally thought I would buy my wedding dress. Eric and I agreed to keep the event casual, and it was the only maternity dress I could find that gave me a somewhat hourglass figure. I felt pretty in it. I turned sideways in front of the standing mirror, and rubbed my hands around my huge protruding belly. I couldn't believe how big I was!

I went into the bathroom and reapplied my makeup. Serena had kindly offered to do my hair and makeup for the day, but I insisted our wedding would be casual and that she come only as a guest.

I very gently put on my colorful haku lei. It was breathtakingly beautiful, and it crowned my new short hair perfectly. My whole outfit was complete, and I felt truly happy staring at my reflection in the mirror.

I heard a light knock on the door.

"Shawnsy, may we come in?"

"Sure, Mom," I said, taking one last look in the mirror.

"Shawnsy, you look absolutely beautiful!" my mom said, coming over and giving me a hug.

"Let me see the bride to be!" Gwen said, giving me a big hug.

"Gwen!" I yelled, so excited to see my sister. "I'm so glad you could make it."

"How could I not come? I'm your maid of honor, and you're my baby sister, of course I would be here for you.

You look beautiful, and you have so many things going on!" she said, holding my hands and looking down at my stomach.

"I know we have so many things to talk about!"

"Michaelann wanted me to give this to you," my mom said, showing me the blue shell necklace.

"That is so pretty. Mom, do you mind putting it on me?" I asked, turning around.

Gwen reached into her purse and twirled a blue garter around her finger. "I thought you could use this for "something blue.""

"Gwen, that's perfect. Thank you so much. But I will definitely need your help putting it on."

"Take a seat," Gwen said pointing to the bed.

I sat back and extended my leg as Gwen rolled it up.

"Let me give you a hand," Gwen said.

We both laughed as she helped me off the bed.

"So when do I get to meet the incredible Eric, who Mom keeps talking about during all our phone calls?"

"Unfortunately, you won't get to talk to him until after the ceremony, but you'll be standing real close to him during the ceremony," I said, glad that Eric and I had decided that his brothers and dad, and my mom, Gwen, Kristen and Michaelann would stand up for us during the ceremony.

"I'm really very happy for you, Shawnsy," Gwen said, giving me another hug.

****

"It's time," I said to myself as I grabbed my bouquet off the dining room table. I opened the deck doors and Eric was there waiting for me. He looked incredibly handsome in a white button down shirt with his sleeves rolled up, and white cotton pants, and a colorful flowered lei draped around his neck.

"You look beautiful," Eric whispered.

"You don't look so bad yourself," I whispered back.

Michaelann had somehow found a singer who also played the ukulele, and he started strumming and singing "Somewhere over the Rainbow." I felt my heart skip a few beats.

Eric turned to me and said, "I think this is our cue."

We walked arm and arm down the aisle. Cameras flashed, and I was beaming with joy as I saw many relatives and friends whom I hadn't seen since my divorce. I saw Alma, Wendy, Rain, Amy and Keisha, all decked out in festive aloha fashion. I laughed to myself at how crazy-cute Keisha, Amy, and Rain looked in their straw skirts. I gave them all a wink as I passed by.

Halfway down the aisle, Vicky and her mom, dressed in classy floral dresses, and our new baby girl, Crystal Faith, met us. Vicky bent down, lifted up the veil covering the white stroller that was adorned with flowers and gently kissed her. Eric and I pushed the stroller the rest of the way down the aisle.

We vowed in front of all of our family and friends, precious daughter and future son that nothing could ever tear us apart, and that we were all a blessed gift to one another. We would honor, love and, above all, respect one another through all the days of our lives. We were then pronounced husband and wife.

Eric and I quickly kissed, and we both bent down and kissed our precious daughter, who was squealing and kicking with delight.

I looked into Eric's eyes and said, "Thank you." Eric's beautiful brown eyes looked deep into mine as he returned the thanks.

The song, "I Can't Help Falling in Love with You," began as Eric picked Crystal Faith up out of the stroller and held her in his arms as we walked back up the aisle as husband and wife.

****

Tiki torches lit up the yard as the day turned into dusk. Michaelann's son, Tony, was the D.J., mixing songs from the 80s and 90s. Stations of fruit and carved meats were set up. Porky Pig was laid out, sporting a pair of sunglasses, which looked like Eric's. A tiki bar with bright blue lights was in the corner, where many of Eric's relatives could be found. Eric and I made the rounds to all our family and friends. As we approached Keisha, Amy, Rain, Alma and Wendy, I felt bittersweet, knowing that it might be a long time before I would see them again.

Eric and I hugged each of them, and I told them how happy we were that they had come. They all doted on Crystal Faith, who was now settled back in her stroller. They loved her little luau dress that was now covered with a thick pink fleece blanket. Tony the D.J. announced that it was time for the first dance. I asked them if they could keep an eye on her for a few minutes as Eric whisked me to the middle of the yard as we clumsily waltzed to "When I Fall in Love." I felt like Cinderella, and Eric was my Prince Charming.

When we were finished dancing, we were met by Vicky and her parents. Vicky and I just hugged as tears welled in her eyes. "Thank you, Shawnsy, and I thank you, Detective McDermott."

Eric gave her a big hug and said, "I promise we will give her a good life."

Vicky nodded her head and smiled.

"We will also let her get away with a lot more because she'll be our little princess," Eric said, trying to lighten the moment.

Vicky's mom hugged Eric, as her dad extended his hand to Eric and said, "Thank you."

Vicky's mom, trying her best to hold it together, hugged me as her husband whispered, "Thank you."

With a shaky voice, Vicky said, "We are going to be heading back home now."

"I understand," I answered. "Why don't all of you go say goodbye to Crystal Faith, she's over there with everyone."

"We will," Vicky said as she started to walk away.

"Vicky, wait," I said suddenly. Vicky turned around.

"I love you, and I truly do thank you."

"Love you, too," Vicky whispered as she walked toward the table.

Eric and I watched as Vicky hugged Alma, Wendy, Amy, Keisha and Rain goodbye. Vicky bent down and stuck her head in the stroller. She had tears streaming down her face as her parents placed their hands on her shoulders for support. A moment later they all walked away.

****

Eric looked at me and said, "I need a drink."

"Me, too," I said, wishing I could have one. We walked over to the tiki bar. Eric and I made quick small talk with everyone standing around as he had a shot. We headed back to the table to reclaim our baby girl.

Tony the D.J. made another announcement: that it was time for all the single ladies to head out to the middle of the yard because it was time for the bouquet to be thrown.

Eric yelled, "Come on, Alma, you're a single lady!"

We all cheered Alma on. Amy and Rain pulled Alma out of her seat.

"You too, Wendy," Eric said.

"Come on, Wendy," Keisha said, pulling her arm.

They all followed me to the middle of the yard, as Eric pushed the stroller. Serena was waiting front and center, looking beautiful in a bright fuschia sundress with one side of her long hair pinned back with stargazer lilies.

"You look beautiful, darling," she said, hugging me. "Congratulations, you found yourself one hot man," she said pointing to Eric, who was pushing the stroller over to my mom and Gwen.

"Thank you, Serena," I said, looking over at Eric.

"Now, remember to throw that thing in my direction," Serena said, taking position.

"I sure will, Serena."

Alma, Wendy, Keisha, Amy, and Rain all surrounded her, along with half a dozen of my single cousins. Beyonce's hit song, "Single Ladies, (Put a Ring on It)," blasted across the yard as I threw the bouquet. Rain and Serena both made a mad dash for it. Everyone around them watched in hysterics to see who would win. Rain grabbed it and held onto it for dear life, laughing and jumping up and down shouting, "I got it! I got it!" Serena, being a good sport, patted Rain on the back and yelled "Nice job!" for all to hear.

A chair was put out for me as Eric showed off his good humor by taking off my sandals and rubbing my swollen feet. He pretended to struggle taking the garter off my leg. He had me laughing so hard I thought I was going to pee. I was so happy when it finally came to an end.

Next, a few of Eric's cousins, dad, and most of his friends from the police department, who by now had taken full advantage of the tiki bar, waited anxiously for the garter to be thrown as "Macho Man" by the Village People began playing. Everyone laughed as a few of them put on their own show by dancing drunk and effeminately to the beat of the music. As Eric threw the garter, a half a dozen of them dove for it. A very drunk former partner of Eric's was the lucky recipient and all of the inebriated men slapped him big high-fives.

Now it was Rain's turn to be the center of attention. Everyone whistled and cheered as "Let's Get It On" by Marvin Gaye was played. The very embarrassed Rain laughed as the garter was placed as far as it could up her leg.

After that, I was hungry and exhausted even though I was having the time of my life. My mom and Gwen still had the baby, and I was glad for the break. Eric and I fixed ourselves a plate, and watched in astonishment as Angus Beef continued to sit in a trance at the laid out Porky Pig.

"There's your mom and sister with the baby. You want to go sit with them?"

"Not right now. I need a breather. Why don't you go, and let Gwen get to know you better?"

"Fine, but don't be surprised if I find out all your childhood secrets."

"Go for it."

As I sat at an empty table, Alma and Wendy came over and joined me. They thanked me for everything as the song "Hot, Hot, Hot" played. Amy led a conga line throughout the yard with Keisha and Rain as the caboose.

"I'm so glad to see them having fun," I said watching them go.

"They sure are. I'm a little worried about Amy, though. I heard her mentioning to Rain that she would like to take off for a few days during the summer," Wendy said.

Alma responded, "Wendy that is her choice. They always have the freedom to leave whenever they want."

"I know, but it's very frustrating," Wendy said.

"What? I can't believe she would even think of leaving! Look what happened before. Where does she plan on going this time?" I asked.

"It seems Rain has been having a lot of contact lately with her cousins, and Amy has been talking with one of her male cousins, but who knows? By the way, Keisha's new school expects her to start in a few weeks," Wendy said.

Suddenly, the three of them came over to us, sweaty and out of breath.

"You guys should have joined the train," Amy said, barely breathing.

"We were having a blast watching all of you," I said.

"Ladies, I believe it's time to say thank you and goodbye," Alma said.

Rain came over and gave me a huge hug. "Bye, Shawnsy, I will miss you."

"I will miss you too, Rain, be good to yourself. Your life is worth it."

Wendy gave me a hug and said, "Shawnsy, don't forget to call us when that baby is born."

"I will definitely let you all know the minute he makes his debut."

"You know where to find me, if you ever need anything," Alma said.

"I know. Thank you, Alma," I said, giving her a quick hug.

I grabbed Keisha's hand and said, "The future is yours, enjoy it, and most importantly don't forget to keep in touch. You have my number if you ever need anything."

"I will, and I will actually be starting my new school in a few weeks."

"I heard! You must be so excited."

"I am, and I promise to keep in touch," Keisha said, giving me a hug. Neither one of us wanted to let go.

I turned to Amy. "Now, Miss Amy, you know I truly want the best for you, and I will always be there for you. I have watched you come so far. I need to know you aren't planning any getaways?"

"Shawnsy, any road I take from now on has to be better than where I've been."

****

"Mom, Brody won't stop teasing me," Crystal Faith said sweetly. She was wearing a pink princess Halloween costume that she refused to put away, even in December. She resembled Vicky so much with her long blonde hair, and sweet demeanor.

I quickly licked the back of the envelope, and turned to Brody. "Please be kind to your sister and let her pretend to be a princess."

"Fine," he said, standing tall in his Batman winter boots. "I want to be just like my Daddy then."

"You already are," I said bending over to give him a kiss. He had Eric's beautiful brown eyes and charming personality.

It has been five years since I left St. Agnes' Place. Eric and I moved to Washington, D.C. after he received a big promotion working for the U.S. Department of Human Trafficking. Eric and I are doing well; he is still not only my husband, but my best friend. He works a lot of hours at his new position, but I am honored to stay home full-time with Crystal Faith and Brody.

Alma and I keep in touch through e-mails. She is still holding down the fort at St. Agnes' Place and seems feistier than ever. Wendy ended up leaving because of the stress, and Alma and I seemed to have lost all contact with her.

Rain eventually left St. Agnes' Place. The last thing Alma had heard about Rain was that she fell off the wagon with drugs, and that she was staying with not-so-savory relatives, who took her in just for the money.

Keisha and I still keep in touch. Eric and I attended her graduation from Boston University, and she recently decided she wants to pursue a degree in law. Currently, she is checking out law schools. Keisha keeps in occasional touch with her mother, who still continues to always be in some form of trouble.

Vicky and I exchange a few letters each year. She had her share of ups and downs, but continued with life much as a normal teenager would once she left St. Agnes' Place. Throughout the years, we exchanged prom pictures and baby photos. In the last letter, she spoke of graduating from nursing school and starting her career as an ER nurse. Someday, I will tell Crystal Faith how she became our daughter, and how brave and beautiful her birth mother really was.

Sadly, Amy did take off once again from St. Agnes' Place, and no one has seen or heard from her since. I pray each day that she is safe and most importantly, happy.

Occasionally, I think of Leelee and wish that I could go back in time and change her past, because maybe then she would be alive today.

I look back fondly and realize, if I had never spent that short period of time at St. Agnes' Place, I would not have the beautiful life I have now.

~The End~

Acknowledgements

I want to thank God for bringing me to a place of happiness and for giving me the words to write.

My wonderful husband, Jamie,

Thank you for encouraging me in all my dreams and for your unwavering love and support. You're the best!

My son, James,

Thank you for sharing the video with me. It meant a lot! I appreciate all the encouragement you have given me. You're the best son ever!

My son, Matthew,

I am so glad we get to share the love of books together. Thank you for encouraging me and letting me invade your game room. You're the best son ever!

My parents,

I thank you from the bottom of my heart for your continuous love and support. You are the best parents anyone could ever ask for!

My two besties, Kristen Stroebel and Karin Gardner,

I thank both of you for the enthusiasm and encouragement that you have given me through each chapter of this book. I am so glad to share this journey with the two of you! xxoo

My dear friend, Jon Stroebel,

You have proven that not all "Jons" are bad! Thank you for being a "first listener."

Michele Villery, my critique partner,

Since I picked up the pen and started writing this book, your encouragement and enthusiasm kept me going through each chapter! I thank you so much!

Lori Hammond, my copy editor,

You are a godsend! I appreciate all the time and energy you have given me.

Wendy Blanchard,

You have amazing talent and I am so blessed to work with you.

To my first readers: my niece Kelly Landers and my dear friend Mickey Bartman,

I thank both of you for your support and enthusiasm from the very beginning!

My aunt, Linda Landers,

You are so loving, kind and beautiful! I thank you from the bottom of my heart for all the love and support you have given me, not only with this book, but with life in general. I love you lots! xxoo

My cousin, Darlene Lawlor,

You're awesome! I thank you from the bottom of my heart for all your help. You're the best!

Judy Blume,

Thank you for opening my eyes as a young girl to the wonderful world of books. You changed my life forever!

To all the people who supported me and this book, I thank you from the bottom of my heart!

~~~~

Resources

Girls Educational & Mentoring Services (GEMS)
www.gems-girls.org

Love 146
P.O. Box 8266
New Haven, Connecticut 06530
Phone Number: 203-772-4420
www.love146.org

National Suicide Prevention Lifeline
1-800-273-TALK (8255)

Jill Starling majored in literature at the State University of New York, Empire State College. Her passions include spending time with her family, writing, reading biographies, watching documentaries, and anything chocolate. She resides in upstate New York with her husband and two young sons.

To find out more about Jill Starling go to
www.JillStarlingnovels.com

Made in the USA
Charleston, SC
24 May 2012